PANDA AND THE KITTY

Furry United Coalition #8

EVE LANGLAIS

Copyright © 2019/20, Eve Langlais

Cover Art by Dreams2Media © 2019

Produced in Canada

Published by Eve Langlais

http://www.EveLanglais.com

E-ISBN: 978 177 384 143 4
Print ISBN: 978 177 384 144 1

"WHO WANTS TO FIGHT?"

The query emerged slightly slurred, indicating the level of drunkenness Jakob had achieved. An admirable state given it took a lot of moonshine to inebriate a shapeshifter —and even more to make a Jones brother drunk.

Shapeshifters metabolized most hard liquor much too quickly. Cost them a fortune to get even the slightest bit tipsy. A good thing that, as a supplier of moonshine to the bar, Jakob drank for free.

As to why he didn't drink at home? That was pathetic even by his standards. Not to mention having more than one drunk Jones in the same vicinity led to some epic black eyes and fat lips. He wasn't in the mood to recover from a concussion-based headache or explain to the cashier at the supermarket why half of his head was shaved—again.

He wouldn't have to worry about his brothers ganging up on him at the Journey's End Tavern, where the worst thing that ever happened was them running out of barbecue peanuts. A sad, sad day, he would add. Nothing beat sucking the flavor from those tiny projectiles and then spitting them at the drunkest fellow in the place for shits and giggles. Watching them slap themselves, assuming it was some kind of bug, always amused.

Other than his fun with peanuts, Jakob tended to behave. He had to since this was a bar catering mostly to humans, and they were fragile compared to him. Couldn't just start a fight with one. Smacking them full strength was out of the question. Pity. He'd been wanting to hit things a lot of late.

His older brother Jackson had informed him he had anger issues. As if! Jackson refused to apologize, even after Jakob repeatedly hit him. Nor did Jakob feel any less angry when he picked a fight with little Jaxon, who was kind enough to scrap with him in an effort to alleviate his frustration.

Jakob had no idea what ailed him. He didn't feel like himself. His bounce had turned to a shuffle. He just didn't get the same enjoyment out of life as he used to.

Something was missing. Not an object though. As a man of few belongings, he'd have noticed if he'd lost any of his few treasures.

Yet, he couldn't help a sense of seeking, looking for what? He didn't quite know.

The door to the bar opened, and a draft of cool evening air slid through, tickling past his nose, bringing with it new scents. Exhaust from a vehicle in the parking lot. A hint of dust—Journey's End sat at the edge of a barren stretch of land. And a perfume he'd only ever smelled once in his life.

He immediately stiffened. It couldn't be her…

Don't look. He was probably wrong. Why would she be here, of all places? He must be mistaken. He dipped his head and stared at his empty glass. Should he order another one? Probably not if he was wasted enough to imagine she'd found him.

Movement by his side caught his attention, and a furtive glance showed a person had ignored the stretch of empty stools to sit beside him. They brought with them a perfume tang and a hint of something else. Not human. Nor the animal he would have expected.

It wasn't *her,* meaning it should have been safe to look.

Jakob turned his head. "Holy jumpin' ants on a hot plate. It *is* you."

He took her in with a single glance. Slender and yet not too tall, elegant in her tailored crimson suit with its smart jacket, blouse, and skirt. Pearls on her lobes and around her neck, her face carefully slathered in makeup to enhance her features, appearing much more sophisticated than he recalled. Her presence tied his tongue. He could think of no brilliant retort. Not to this woman.

She didn't have the same issue. "Hello, son."

"Mother," was his short and sour reply.

Jakob didn't like giving her that solemn title. But what else could he call Mrs. Veronica Guinevere Jones, mother of five, who'd abandoned her family when he was just a boy? Broke his father's heart. Poor man had been consoling himself with lady after lady since he'd been dumped. Truly horrible all the sex Da indulged in to try and feel better.

Jakob didn't know how he did it. When Jakob's one and only true love ditched his ass and threatened to set it on fire, the few flings he'd had left him feeling hollow and dirty. It was true what they said. A man never forgot his first love.

"Well, are you going to talk or sulk?" Mother

demanded in an annoyed tone she had no right taking. None at all.

He glared at his mum. "I ain't got nothing to say to you." Unlike some of his other brothers, he didn't wallow in the mire of emotions that came from being abandoned. Rather than mope, he chose to be angry.

"Are you sure about that? I would have said you had plenty to ask me." Mrs. Veronica Guinevere Jones—or would that be Malone since, technically, the marriage was considered over—half turned on the stool to face him.

She used to tuck him into bed and kiss his forehead before heading back to the living room to spend the next hour or more yelling at his da about how unhappy she was because he had no goals. It was almost a nightly thing. Sometimes it ended in the door slamming shut and the spinning of wheels on gravel as his da took off for the evening, unable to make his wife happy.

Other nights, his dad knew the right things to say and his parents had sex. Nine months later...hello, new brother. Jakob wouldn't have minded a sister. A sister probably wouldn't have beaten him with claims she was toughening him up like his older brothers did.

Jakob eyed her, a woman who'd been so unhappy she faked her own death to escape her family. Did he really want to fall down a crocodile hole asking why? Could he really pass up the chance to hear the bullshit excuse she'd use?

"Why did you do it?"

"Do you mean the interview with the media? I thought it was time to tell the world that humans aren't the dominant species like they thought." Her lips curved into a smile that held a hint of the serpent from the garden that corrupted.

"Hunh?" He blinked. "I actually think it's funny you went on television and claimed you believed in shapeshifters."

With cameras popping up everywhere, and social media spreading news like wildfire, it was only a matter of time before they were outed. Better to do it by gentle announcement than because someone caught a meat eater chomping on a human culled from the herd—or so his Uncle Kyle claimed.

"If you agree with what I'm doing, then you know why I did it. It's time our kind stopped hiding."

"Whatever. Don't really care. That's not what I was asking about, though. I meant, why did you leave us?" Asked with impatience that hopefully masked any sign of pathetic-ness. It felt weak to ask, and worse, he was anxious for a reply. Why did she do it? Was it his fault? Could he have done something different so his mum wouldn't have left him?

Was he so unlovable?

Ugh. The emotions. He thought his mommy issues were buried. He'd have to beat them back into hiding later. Maybe get his hands on some more moonshine.

As it turned out, his mother's reason had nothing to do with him at all. "I left because I was destined for greater things." She pronounced it as if it were the most logical thing for a mother of five to do to her children.

"You made us believe you were dead!" As jaded as he was, he still had the capacity for shock.

She'd made them all believe she'd died in a dingo attack when he was just a knee-high lad still. Jakob and his brothers did their best to eradicate the hollow feeling that came from losing their mum, the only voice of sanity in their house. With her gone, they had no one to stop them

5

from climbing things they shouldn't. Blowing up shit. Fighting with their fists, then weapons. Joining a secret paramilitary operation. The adrenaline used to carry him; now he longed for a quieter pace of life.

Maybe he'd do something drastic and crazy like get hitched. His brothers who'd tied the knot seemed happy enough.

"I needed a clean break."

"Ever hear of divorce?" was his sarcastic reply.

"Are you really going to whine and cry about it? It happened. Get over it. You're reminding me why I left the sniveling lot of you."

"And this would be why you never won mother of the year."

"I would have been better off if I'd drowned the lot of you at birth."

The blow of her statement snapped his psyche into stunned shock. Anyone else he would have punched. He couldn't hit a woman, let alone his mother. Why did she have to come back? He was better off when he thought her dead. "What is wrong with you?"

"I assume you're still being tiresome and referring to the fact I lack a maternal gene. What can I say? Children bore me." She shrugged.

"You could say 'I'm sorry.'"

Laughter trilled from her. "But I'm not. Or do you want me to lie?"

Ouch. Rather than wince, he signaled Anvil, who slid him a fresh glass of booze before heading to the back of the bar. Jakob took a swig that went down like water. "If you feel nothing, then why are you here?"

"To see you, of course."

He didn't let the little boy inside feel any excitement at her words. He doubted she'd come for a reconciliation. And why him? Why not one of his older, more stable brothers? Or his da? "What do you want?"

"Such a complicated question. Would it help if I said my final goal is world domination?" She said it with a pretty smile as if it weren't the most ludicrous thing ever.

He blinked. "The humans won't ever let you be in charge."

"You are assuming I'd let them have a choice. And who says there will be any humans left to get in my way?"

"Did you just imply genocide?" He couldn't even believe the words passed his lips. Who was this person? Not his mother. That was for sure. Not a Jones either.

"Stated, actually. It is a known fact the world is over-populated and that the climate crisis is being caused by humans."

"Actually, according to some scientists, it's a planetary rotational axis thing, not carbon."

"Humans are still a blight upon this world, and we'd be better off without them."

"You're talking about murdering billions of people. It will never happen."

"Who said anything about killing them? There is more than one way to ensure humans stop being the dominant species."

"How?" He was curious about her obviously psychotic manifesto.

"You know what they say. If you can't beat them, change them."

"Have you been sniffing glue? You can't change humans into shifters."

"That's what you think. And not just humans. Imagine if we weren't stuck with what we were born with. What if we could be better? Stronger?"

As she spoke, something about her relaxed and her scent shifted. His eyes widened as he grasped what she implied. "You've used Mastermind's serum."

Mastermind was an evil creature who'd devoted her time to concocting potions to enhance certain attributes in shifters, only it went horribly wrong. A pity Mastermind's ideas and recipes didn't die when she did.

"Please." She snorted. "That pipsqueak only ever managed failures. Unstable concoctions with wild effects, whereas I"—Veronica's smile turned devious—"have created a compound that is highly directed and effective with the right candidate."

"What do you mean you created? I never knew you were a chemist." When he was growing up, she appeared constantly appeared frazzled trying to keep up with a massive household of boys on a stretched budget.

"Because I let hormones get in the way. I went to college, you know, on a scholarship. Top of my class until your dad impregnated me. The cad promised I could go back to school after the babe was born, only there was no time, no money, and the damned babies kept coming."

"Ever hear of birth control?" He rolled his eyes.

"Back then, the weak versions on the market didn't work on shifters, and I was ridiculously fertile."

"So to pursue your dream of being a mad scientist, you abandoned your family."

"I was left with no choice. I needed to be free to fulfill my destiny." Again, she had no apology.

"That's a load of dingo crap," he muttered. "When we

found you, a while back, in that secret lab, you were hooked up with that Wilson fellow." Kole Wilson, an evil koala shifter whom everyone thought was the true power behind the continued experiments on shifters. The only good thing that came out of that mission was his brother hooked up with that Nev chick. The bad? They realized their mother was a real twat.

"Kole was useful to my goals."

"Meaning he was rich," Jakob spat.

"Filthy rich," she said with a smirk. "And when Kole died, guess who inherited everything?"

A reminder the evil koala had perished for his actions while Jakob's mother managed to slip away.

"Guess you got everything you wanted," was his sour reply.

"I did." She seemed determined to keep verbally kicking him down.

Jakob swallowed more moonshine, but it didn't help. His drunkenness had faded into stone-cold sobriety. "Did you come here just to rub my face in the fact you're a shit mum? Or did you have another reason?"

"I need your help with something."

"As if I'd help you," he sneered. "I wouldn't waste a piss on you, even if you were on fire."

She went on as if he'd not said a thing. "I need to send a message to the shifter council."

"Send it yourself. I'm sure they're dying to talk to you." Probably anxious for a location so they could remove the threat. The problem being, how to take out a woman who'd gone from pretending she was dead to the star of the hour in the human limelight? They had to remove her without drawing the wrong kind of attention.

If she were anyone else, Jakob would have instigated a bar fight and solved the threat to his family. He only needed one punch. *Kapow.* Not many could get up from his version of the TKO, not without medical help at least.

But he was tired of being a weapon.

And she was his mom.

"Before I give the council my demands, I need them to understand why I'm to be obeyed."

He snorted. He couldn't help it. "No one is going to obey you."

"Because they think I'm weak." A reference to her lowly position in shifter society. There were two kinds of shifters: predator and prey. Although these days, the prey blended in better with society, given those who resorted to violence didn't do so well when they caught the attention of humans. "Wait until they see what I can do."

"You?" He snickered. Given his mum shifted into a quokka—a marsupial the size of a house cat—the only living things that feared her were the grass and leaves. Quokkas were known to be the cutest creatures with the nicest disposition. Usually. His mother bucked that trend.

"You shouldn't mock me. You have no idea what I'm capable of."

"Killing people with cuteness? Ooh, scary." He fake shuddered and laughed. "Maybe if you turned into a bus-sized version, you might be a little dangerous."

Judging by her expression, she didn't like the insult. "For your information, I learned how to switch size and add body parts after the first rendition of the formula. However, it is my latest accomplishment that the council will be most concerned about."

"Oh yeah, what did you do?"

"So glad you asked because you're about to find out."

Ominous words that made him laugh. "Is this where you ask me to go to the parking lot with you so I can see you transform? I ain't going anywhere with you."

"That's what you think. You have a choice to make. Come with me quietly, or by force."

"Force?" He eyeballed her and her smart suit. She could make all the claims she wanted. He was a trained kangaroo fighter. A predator despite what some might think. "You should have brought your army."

"Who says I didn't?"

The human bar still remained full of humans, about a dozen or so scattered all around. But as his mother raised her hand, the music cut out and all the voices went quiet. Too many eyes watched. Jakob slid off his stool to stand.

"Enlisting the aid of humans?" he asked softly. "I thought your plan was to get rid of them." He hoped to keep her distracted a moment while he reassessed.

"Are they human, though? Take another sniff." Veronica swiveled on her seat and cocked her head as she waited.

He wanted to walk out and yet found himself taking a deep breath. The scents were as he'd expect in a bar—beer, liquor, peanuts, and wood from the furniture and floors. The patrons were a mix of sweat, soap, cologne, and... He frowned. There was something else, something that made no sense.

"They all smell the same."

"The problem with having them all dosed out of the same batch. But nonetheless, still effective, don't you think?"

"You did something to mask their scent."

"And replace it with another. That's the one good I got out of that mistake of a marriage. Access to your family's recipe books. A little bit of that with some science added to the mix and poof!" She snapped her fingers. "The spray sells for a pretty penny."

"Hold on a second. You sell the human cologne?"

Veronica leaned against the bar and smirked. "Among other things. It takes a lot of funds to finance the kind of research I want to do. I knew early on I'd need a way of making money."

"Which is why you hooked up with Kole?"

She snorted. "Kole barely had any money to his name. What he had was connections. I made the money. Early on I realized we'd need a large sum to do our work. We invested in designer perfumes. Scents chemically balanced to individuals, taking their natural pheromones into consideration and crafting something unique."

He didn't need her to say anymore. "You made a cologne to hide a shifter's scent." His gaze flicked to the humans still standing, still watching him.

"Hide it. Change it. Enhance it. Amazing what a smell can do."

She sounded quite proud.

"It's…" He wanted to say all kinds of things, and yet, he was a man who appreciated good camouflage. "Brilliant."

Her lips parted in a surprised smile. "Thank you. It's been quite effective not only in funding the research but in getting the people I need into the right places. We must get ready."

"For what?"

"Join me and find out," she offered.

"You have to be kidding. Join you as a minion of darkness? Ha. Never. And now that you've divulged your plan, I'm going to have to ask you to come with me." He reached into his inner vest pocket and pulled out his wallet, flipping it open to display his badge that showed his status with the Furry United Coalition. "Official FUC agent and you are under arrest for being a danger to shifter society."

"You don't say?" She appeared amused. "Funny because I'm the one who is actually going to save it. It's only a matter of time before humans come after us. We need to be ready."

"The council—"

"Is useless. They're being too cautious, and it will come back to bite them. I won't let their inaction doom us all. They will bow to my demands or face the consequences."

"You're insane."

"That's what they always say of those who embrace greatness. But you'll see. Everyone will thank me when I save us from being annihilated by the humans."

"Co-existence is possible."

"They can't even live amongst each other," his mother retorted. "You're obviously not too bright. The lot of you always did take more after your father's side than mine."

"Thank you. I'd hate to think we're anything like you." He tossed the insult.

Her lips thinned in displeasure. "If you're done proving your ignorance, then it's time to go."

"I'm not going anywhere with you."

"Then by force it is." She lifted a hand, and a pair of the patrons neared.

Jakob dropped into a loose fighting stance.

Anvil chose that moment to return, carrying a case of booze. He took the situation in and barked, "Not in my bar." He set down the case with a thump and pulled out his bat from under the counter. "Don't even think of starting trouble."

His mother tossed bills onto the counter. "We're leaving now."

Anvil tapped the bat against his open palm. "Sounds like a good idea. But you're not taking him." He angled his head at Jakob.

"Actually, we are," Veronica replied with a wide smile. "And you're coming, too."

"Listen, lady, he might be too nice to hit you, but I'm not." Anvil grinned, showing off his gold tooth.

"Another one who thinks with his fists." She shook her head. "Talk about a messy way of doing things."

"Did you really think you wouldn't have to fight?" Jakob asked.

"Oh, I expected it, which is why my people came armed." Weapons emerged and were split between aiming at Jakob and Anvil.

"Bullets? That's not very sporting of you," he said, calculating his odds to be poor against that many guns.

"They're not going to kill you, dear son. On the contrary, I need you alive. Put them to sleep," she commanded, dropping her hand.

Jakob threw himself to the side, but there was no way to avoid the fifteen or so darts that came flying his way.

Instant sluggishness filled his veins. He didn't even have time to finish muttering, "Bitch," before he was sagging.

JAKOB WOKE UP FACE FIRST IN THE DUST OUTSIDE THE

compound gate that provided access to his home. Having eaten that dust before, he recognized the taste.

It took some doing and lots of groaning to get to his feet. He wavered as he blinked away the fatigue. Last thing he recalled was someone shooting him with sleeping darts. Then nothing. He'd obviously passed out or gone into some fugue state that allowed him to make it out of the bar and back home. It must have been an epic battle, if only he could remember it.

He staggered up the drive toward the house, feeling disconnected from his body. Stupid, too. Rather than chatting with his mum, he should have found a way to contact backup. Imagine the coup if he'd managed to help bring her ass in for questioning.

The house appeared up the drive, and he shuffled faster. He couldn't wait to flop into his bed. Apparently, his arrival didn't go unnoticed. A welcoming committee poured out the door, a bunch of male bodies jostling and pushing to get to Jakob first.

"Little brother!"

"You bastard!"

"Where have you been?"

The medley of voices shouted at him, making him grab his spinning head. He felt strange, his mind sluggish.

His family kept yapping and, oddly, touching him. Patting him. Checking him over.

"Would you all calm down? I'm fine." If hungover, which was a rarity for him.

"Fine! Where have you been all this time?" His father's query cut through the din.

It was then he took in a few details, such as the haggard expression on some of the faces, the beard Jackson sported, which he'd not had the day before. The very round and pregnant belly sported by his sister-in-law. How had that happened overnight?

It took a few more seconds before he put all the pieces together enough to ask, "How long have I been gone?"

"Three and a half months."

2

Months…

As Jakob did his best to grasp that concept, he was bustled inside. Overwhelmed by the noise and commotion, he teetered on his feet and grabbed his head.

Da was the one to declare, "The boy needs his bed."

Hands grabbed and pretty much carried him to his room. Everyone crowded inside, staring.

Jakob swayed.

His dad snapped, "Everyone, git."

No one dared argue, meaning Jakob got a moment of quiet to collapse onto his bed and close his eyes. When he woke, it was to a warm broth steaming on a tray at the foot of his bed and his da still in the room, sitting beside him.

Only after Jakob drank down the nutrient-rich soup did his father ask, "What happened?"

"Mum."

One word and yet he might as well have slugged his da. His face blanched. After that, it took only a moment to relate everything that happened. Up until Jakob was tranked. Then…nothing.

"You've been gone for over three months," his da said softly. "We had no idea if you were dead or alive. We only heard about your truck being left in the Journey's End parking lot because the coppers gave us a shout when they found it after the fire."

"What fire?"

"The one someone set in the bar. They've been looking for you and Anvil to ask questions. Their theory is you set the fire on purpose to collect insurance money and skipped town together."

"She was covering her tracks," he grumbled.

"Aye. We know that now." His da scrubbed his face. "I'm sorry."

"For what?"

His da, usually so big and brash, hunched. "For everything. I should have never married your mum. I knew she wasn't happy. But I kept trying."

"She hates us." He would never admit the twinge at saying it aloud.

"Aye. But I don't." His father pulled him close for a hug. "You ready to see the rest of the family?"

Not really, but he knew if the roles were reversed, he'd want reassurance that the other person was okay. Jakob emerged from his room into a kitchen of chaos with brothers, wives, and uncles all over the place. Not many cousins though. Da was the only Jones senior to actually settle down and have a large family.

Given all the personalities in the room, it took some time before Jakob managed to tell everyone his story. Which then led to some even livelier discussions. All through it, Jakob remained mostly quiet, apart. It was his Uncle Kendrick who noticed it.

"The boy looks like he's going to pass out."

Actually, he puked. A lot. And ran a fever, a rarity given one of the benefits of being a shapeshifter was exceedingly good health. Yet for seventy-two hours after he was returned to his family, he was hacking and coughing, his eyes bleary, his fever spiking. He was convinced he would die. Especially since he couldn't shapeshift. Hadn't been able to since his return from his forgotten sojourn in the unloving bosom of his mother, and not for a lack of trying on his part.

His scent also changed, with his brothers muttering amongst each other that he didn't smell the same. He actually gave off a human vibe.

"Liar!" he said, swinging a weak fist that Jackson didn't even try to avoid. Dizzy from illness and the knowledge something was very wrong with him, he'd run from the room. On two legs, without a single hop. Nothing worse than being a kangaroo that couldn't bounce. Couldn't fight either.

While he knew in theory how to spar with his fists, he lacked the agility and power of before. The uncanny ability to dodge and mete out punishment had been puked out along with stuff he was pretty sure he'd last eaten a decade ago. His weakened status led to his brothers going easy on him. Worse, they pitied him.

But no worse than he pitied himself.

He told his story numerous times, everyone having almost the same reaction to Mum's perfidy.

His big brother Jackson ranted most of all. "That lying—"

Uncle Kevyn slapped his hand over Jackson's mouth before he could say something really rude.

"What did she do to you?" was the most pressing question everyone wondered, including Jakob.

The family called in some favors and had him checked out by a doctor, who declared him perfectly fit. The blood-work showed him as healthy, everything in the proper ranges. Even his DNA appeared normal…for a human.

When Uncle Kyle revealed their medical findings, Jakob had blinked. "Human? What do you mean I'm human?" He stared at his hands. They looked the same. His feet. His body. Everything looked as it should; it just lacked that something special he used to count on.

"She did something to you, boy." His father looked apologetic, whereas his brothers and uncles appeared horrified.

He understood the feeling.

Human. It explained why he couldn't shift.

After that, things went downhill. For Jakob at least. He started drinking and easily getting drunk. A drunk and depressed Jones meant he picked a lot of fights. Lost more than a few now that he was as mundane as the rest of them. He missed his bouncy half. He spent hours on the first full moon staring at the silver orb, hoping to sprout fur, anything.

But it was gone. The thing that made him special, gone.

Because she'd taken it.

That was the message she wanted him to give the council. However, Jakob was an ornery bastard. Rather than give his wretched mother the satisfaction of doing her bidding, he moved out of the compound. He wanted to live on his own for a while, somewhere he wouldn't be a source of pity to anyone—and so he could continue the hunt for his mother in peace, something his family had discouraged. They used the words "obsessed" and "self-destructive." They didn't understand.

She'd betrayed him. Again.

Worse, she'd taken the thing that defined him. His other half. His animal soul. He was nothing without it.

Jakob had to do something, and he had to do it alone. Jackson threatened to break his legs to keep him home, but desperation compelled Jakob to leave. He couldn't stand being surrounded by the familiar and feeling as if he didn't belong.

Not to mention, he had a mission; locate his mother and make her put his kanga back!

Finding his mum wasn't as easy as expected, given she'd disappeared again. Something she proved to be quite adept at. It didn't help that he'd cut off his family and wouldn't call in any favors. He didn't want to share his shame with anyone.

Woe is me. His depression played the world's smallest violin quite well, and for the first time in his life, he actually managed to gain weight as he tried to eat away his blues.

As if it wasn't bad enough he was just a human now, he sported a gut and couldn't even walk the mile to the store for beer without gasping for breath. But in good news, it was much cheaper now for him to get drunk.

It was during his huffing and puffing jaunt to the pizza parlor that he got distracted by something that smelled even yummier than tomato sauce, baked cheese, and crispy pepperoni.

"What's that smell?"

The intriguing scent drew him into a furniture store of all places, and he followed his nose to a table. Not a big one either, the small kind meant to put your coffee cup on, or maybe roll a joint. He knew nothing about name brands or detail work or any of the crap that a true furniture aficionado might be privy to. He didn't actually need any furniture, although, while he was here, he really should look at getting a new mattress. His last one had developed a disturbing dent in it.

However, he couldn't take his eyes off the table. His hand went to his pocket, the fabric one in his shirt, not the one he used to have by his belly. He pulled out a cigarette but retained enough wits to not light it. A nasty habit and yet he'd started it again because it suited his mood. Just like the city suited him right now with its dark alleys and seedy underground.

Of late, he'd been barely leaving his place, his rage having finally calmed down enough that he missed home. Missed his annoying brothers, his well-meaning but often wrong uncles. His father who said if life hit you in the chin, get up and hit it back.

Might be time to go for a visit and go a few rounds in the gym. Knock a few teeth and rattle some bones.

Nothing better than hitting something for some relief. He could use some relief, especially of late. In this past week, he'd felt odd. Itchy in his skin, lacking any hunger for his usual favorites, which truly let him know something was amiss. It was why he'd decided to grab himself a pizza. Surely he'd find his appetite with a fresh pepperoni delight?

His belly rumbled, but not for a baked pie. Jakob dropped to his knees by the wooden side table and sniffed.

Mmm. Definitely yummy smelling. He stroked his hands over the smoothness. Admired the texture, the taste…

"Excuse me, sir, but are you licking that accent table?"

It was a bit shocking to realize yes, as a matter of fact, he was licking the table.

That was a first. He leaned back on his heels and

sought a reason for his odd behavior. "Just, er, testing the impermeability of the veneer you chose."

"Sure, you were," said the salesman, drawing out the words.

"What kind of wood is this?" Jakob noted its pale grain and interesting knots. They tempted his fingertips, and he couldn't help but stroke it. His mouth watered.

"This finely crafted product is made from bamboo."

What he knew of bamboo didn't jive with the table. "Isn't that like a tiny stick? How can they make furniture with it?"

The salesman shrugged, and interestingly enough, his lush seventies mustache wiggled as well. "From what I know, they glue the strips together. It's considered to be an environmentally friendly choice given how rapidly it grows."

"How much for it?" Because the licking hadn't curbed his interest in it.

Even the price tag over seven hundred dollars—for a table that weighed less than the ham in his fridge—didn't deter him. His credit card cried a little as he swiped it, but he exited the store the new owner of a bamboo side table— which he had no room for. He currently lived in a cramped bachelor pad that came with built-in furniture. His home for the past few weeks. Perhaps buying the table was a sign he should move on?

He strapped it to the top of his environmentally friendly smart car, on loan from the garage that was fixing his Dodge Ram pickup truck. The tiny vehicle embarrassed him to the extreme. Real men didn't drive around in teeny, tiny electric cars. They drove over them and crushed them with their monster trucks.

But as with everything else right now in his life, his

manly truck had broken down, and he was stuck feeling out of place behind the wheel and everywhere else.

Where did he belong? Seeing his mother had only made that question worse. Maybe if he found her, he would find an answer. And get his kanga back!

Jakob carried his new prize into his ground floor apartment. It had only the one door going in and out and one moderate-sized window. It wasn't the homiest of places.

He missed the country. City living looked a lot more fun on television. In truth, he hated the lack of greenery. He longed for his connection to the wilderness.

He set the table on the counter before sitting on the only chair in his apartment to stare at it. Now that he had it here, he was even more baffled. He had no need of an accent side table. Yet, he'd bought the overpriced thing.

He poked it. Ran his hand over the smooth wood. Next thing he knew, he was licking it again. Not just slobbering all over it but trying to bite the wood. He'd already gnawed off the veneer in some places. Shocking, and yet it didn't curb his craving. He wanted to chew on it some more.

Obviously, his diet was lacking in something. Now, some people might have chosen at this point to go see a doctor to get their blood tested. Or even hit a pharmacy or health food store for vitamins.

Rather than do any of those things, Jakob grabbed the table and slammed it down on the floor. In no time at all, he had seven-hundred-dollar splinters. He went to bed with a belly full of bamboo and slept sixteen hours.

The next day, a specialty shop sold him some fresh bamboo shoots, and he bought the crunchy juicy ones in cans. He spent that day gorging, lying on the floor of his apartment, stalks and tin cans splayed around him, happy as could be and was ready for a nap when he heard a noise outside.

Probably rats. They thrived on the waste people in the city tossed out. And if you tried to stop them... they tore apart your shit looking for discarded treats. Jakob knew better than to fight them on it. He left them all the dinner scraps, plus some extra, and in return, the rats didn't raid his home looking for food. It was a form of blackmail really, but given getting rid of scraps meant less garbage and flies, it worked out rather well for them both.

From the chunks of bamboo by his side, Jakob snared a piece with a dark knot in it and wondered if it would taste different. He was just crunching into the interesting spot when he heard a thump overhead.

Not unheard of given he had neighbors.

He popped a piece of wood into his mouth and rolled to his feet. He chewed the tasty bit as he opened the dishwasher and pulled out a rather large gun. He also slipped two full magazines in his pockets along with a smoke bomb.

Many people in the books and movies had this misconception about shifters, mainly that they only relied on their beast when it came to fighting.

False.

Shifters knew better than to unleash their animal side in public. Places where they might be discovered were best served with guns and subterfuge.

Weapon in hand, he waited. When his door handle turned, he fired through it then dropped to the ground.

There was no return fire.

Interesting. They wanted him alive. The question being, how many had they sent?

A voice, projected through a bullhorn, yelled, "This is

Detective Lawrence with the fifty-first law enforcement district. Come out with your hands up."

Cops? Who in the blazing hells called the cops on him? And why?

"You got the wrong apartment," he yelled.

"Are you Jakob Jones?"

Shoot. Right apartment. He didn't reply and instead dove for his phone, only to curse when he saw he had no signal. He wouldn't be calling for help. He glanced at the ceiling. Did he have time to cut through it and get to another level?

The door blasted open, and he fired high so as to not accidentally hit any humans because then he'd be in real trouble. He emptied the clip as he charged for the opening, feeling his body adrenalizing.

And wait, was that a spark as his body contorted as if ready to shift. Oh shit. The timing couldn't have been worse.

He did his best to keep it stuffed, but his animal self shoved to dominate.

"Not now," he rumbled as his skin started to stretch. He couldn't hold it in!

Hide. He had to hide, somehow. He fumbled for the smoke bomb and tossed it. Just in time, as he felt his body morphing as he went through the door.

"Grawr!" His battle cry was deep and gruff as he emerged into the apartment complex's courtyard, shrouded in lung-burning smoke. He chose a direction and charged, moving past the hanging cloud. It went from dark to really bright and not because of any sunlight. There were so many lights shining on him, making him blink as he tried to adjust.

He could hear yelling. "Shoot it! Take that thing down."

Thing? How rude!

"Watch for Jones. The animal is probably a diversion."

Aha. So they didn't suspect. He should try and escape. He went to hop, only to fall forward. He felt more at ease on his hands and feet, which was weird. A kanga always bounced on its hind legs.

He'd worry about it later. He had to escape. He feinted toward a group of officers clustered at the entrance to the courtyard. One of them fired.

Thwack.

He recognized the sting.

Tranquilizers? Again?

Was this his mother's doing? Had she enlisted the police? Another dart struck him and another. These were smaller than the ones his mother used. Much smaller with low doses.

Rather than put him to sleep, they dulled his senses. His usually harmonious beast side pushed for full control. It seemed just easier to let it do as it wanted.

Let's bounce out of here. It was what he meant to do. Yet he soon realized he was running on four legs, not two. People were screaming, "Oh my God, he's huge."

"Holy shit, it's a bear."

Damned tourists, not recognizing his kanga greatness.

"Look at him. He's so cute!"

A sentiment he appreciated as he broke through the chain of tranquilizer-toting humans in full riot gear and went galloping off down the city streets.

He'd be in so much trouble with the council. More than likely, they'd send him a few FUC's to straighten him out. Maybe some ASS, too, for a proper spanking.

It wasn't until he made it outside of the city and collapsed by a stream that he finally saw what his mother had done.

He wasn't a human as he'd feared. It was worse. So much worse.

The reflection in the river didn't show a handsome 'roo staring back at him. But a cute and roly-poly furry panda bear face.

Nooooooo!

3

THE FOOTAGE of the panda bear racing off into the city played on every channel. Speculation abounded, some stating it was a hoax, that the fuzzy shape that burst out of an apartment complex through a cloud of smoke was never an animal to start with but someone dressed as one.

Some thought it was a bear all along, panicked because it had been trafficked into the country and held in a confined prison. The animal activists were screaming bloody murder about the heavily armed cops who showed up and scared the poor defenseless bear, who'd tossed aside the humans like they were bowling pins when he charged through them and trampled the hood of a police car forming the perimeter.

And then there some television hosts asking if this was proof that shapeshifters existed. It didn't help that this incident occurred months after the revelation by Mrs. Jones that werewolves were only the tip of the iceberg when it came to shit humans didn't know.

The ex-Mrs. Jones, mother to a boy Maisy used to date,

had risen from the dead and, to save her own skin, divulged their secret. Then she'd gone into hiding.

The shifter Council—and that was Council with a capital C—was in an uproar, with good reason. The revelation, even if ridiculed, endangered all of shifter kind—or, as some of the older groups called them, skinwalkers. Maisy's grandad always hated the name, which had gained popularity in the last decade as stories emerged with shifters as heroes and villains. Heck, one of the biggest names in romance was writing from experience, and the Council would have sanctioned her except for the fact she bribed her way onto a seat.

No matter the name used to describe them—or how many rippled abs adorned book covers—the world wasn't ready for cryptids to emerge. Not ready for what they deemed "monsters."

Mrs. Jones didn't care. The Council and shifters around the world went into defensive mode. Nobody wanted the humans to come looking for them with shotguns and pitchforks. The Council's hackers went into overdrive, wiping anything that might prove their existence and planting seeds of doubt everywhere they could. There was an entire Reddit thread on the fact Mrs. Jones had hired a special effects person to perpetrate the hoax.

To everyone's relief, Mrs. Jones's attempt to reveal their existence failed.

And then the rampaging panda video emerged just over two weeks ago.

Maisy had no doubt the Council had people already working on debunking it. To make people doubt their own eyes. But Maisy knew the truth. What she didn't understand was how Jakob got involved. His name was bandied about by the police as a person of interest. Interest in what? No one would say, but his face ended up plastered everywhere.

The host on the news program returned after the clip finished playing, his expression serious as he said, "Truth or lie? What do you think?"

The screen then flipped to Mrs. Jones at her press conference, where she looked right in the camera and said, "Shapeshifters are your neighbors and friends."

Yes, they were. Which was why the television host asked the provocative and dangerous question, "How can we protect ourselves from the monsters?"

The people scrambling to buy silver thought they knew. But in reality, a bullet would shoot a person dead even if they could swap into fur. Strangle, shoot, dismember, poison. Shapeshifters weren't immortal. She would know since she doctored them.

Maisy flipped off the telly and its drama. She had no need of it. She rather liked her life as it was. Quiet. Predictable.

Boring...

A brisk knock at her door raised her head. Only one reason for anyone to be coming to her this late at night. Someone needed her help.

As the only healer for shifters for hundreds of miles around, she often got calls at odd times. An ostrich who'd gotten an egg stuck playing erotic games. A hyena so depressed it lost its laugh. A hard case to fix until they'd discovered the hormonal imbalance. Now Tricia was laughing all the time, usually at the expense of others.

No matter the case, Maisy did her best to offer a cure.

Wrapping her sweater more tightly around her body,

she ignored the bristling of her inner feline and grabbed the the walking stick with its pointed metal tip. Saving lives was one thing. Protecting herself, another. She wasn't dumb. She lived by herself in the middle of nowhere.

Pausing behind her door, a thick wooden affair that could withstand even the rampaging kick of a kanga, she leaned close and said, "Who is it?"

The reply, just one word, sent a chill through her.

"Jakob."

She opened her mouth to tell him to leave. She wasn't ready to deal with him yet. She might never be ready. He'd broken her heart, and while it had been a while ago, time hadn't healed that wound. Not to mention, he was a wanted man. She didn't need that kind of trouble.

But then he said the magic words she couldn't ignore. "I need help."

She flung open the door and gaped at him. For one thing, he looked haggard, his skin a terrible shade, his eyes wide and bloodshot, and he was sweating. Profusely.

No matter what she thought of him, the side that had sworn to help people kicked in. "Jakob, what happened to you?"

"I got jumped."

"Obviously." But he wouldn't have come to her with just bruises and broken bones. "Get inside, and while I clean you up, you can tell me about it."

She stepped to her left, and he staggered in, making her note he'd gotten thicker since she'd last seen him. The chub around his middle suited him. He'd always been a touch on the skinny side. Not anymore.

He might even be a tad too heavy. He flung himself onto the couch, and it groaned ominously. He glared at the bright-colored cushions.

She sat across from him on the low coffee table, hands on her knees. "Jakob, what's going on?"

"Something is wrong with me."

"Can you tell me where it hurts?" Because, despite the roughness of his exterior, she saw no gaping wounds or bent limbs.

"That's just it; it doesn't hurt. And yet it should, because it's horrible. You have to fix it, Maze." He turned a wild gaze on her. "Promise me you'll fix it."

"Fix what?" she asked, distracted by the nickname only he used. "I don't see anything that needs mending. No blood. No broken bones."

"That's because I'm holding it in. I won't let it escape. It wants to. It knows you'll coo and aah over the cuteness of it. You'll want to pet it. And I won't be able to stop you."

The more he spoke, the more she got angry as she gauged his intent. "Did you seriously come banging on my door to get me to touch your *thang*?" She glared at him. Not that she would mind. Jakob always knew how to make her purr in bed. It was the fact he didn't love her that hurt.

"Who said anything about sex? Wait, would you have sex?" he asked rather hopefully. He shook his head a second later. "Don't distract me. This is serious. We can't have sex. Not until you fix me."

"Again, fix what? Spit it out. What's wrong with you?"

His expression held a hint of horror as he whispered, "I'm a panda."

She took a moment to digest this and then snapped, "Am I some kind of joke to you?"

"Never!" he exclaimed. "I came to you because you're the only one I trust."

"You are not a panda." Although she would admit he needed a shower because he didn't smell like himself. Given her sense of smell was poor compared to others, that said a lot.

"I wish that were true, but she changed me. I'm not a 'roo anymore. I'm a cute and cuddly bear!" His anguish was too real to be feigned.

She reached to palpate his forehead. "You're not running a fever. Have you ingested any mushrooms or herbs in the last twenty-four hours? Maybe smoked or smelled something odd?"

"I'm not high. My mother did this. She's somehow taken my 'roo."

"That's impossible," she sputtered. "No one can take your animal and replace it with another."

"Oh, really? Have you forgotten what Mum was doing?" was his long-drawled reply. He reminded her of Nev, a human woman who ended up sporting wings, a new species that only a few dared whisper: harpy.

"It's one thing to change latent humans into a hybrid species, another to completely rip out your beast and replace it with another."

He winced. "Must you say rip?"

"Well, you did say it hurt."

"Not that kind of hurt. This kind." He thumped his chest. "It hurts almost as much as when you dumped me."

A part of her reveled in the fact he admitted he'd felt something. "Am I supposed to feel sorry for you? You deserved it."

"For doing what? Serving my country like a good citizen?" His voice rose as his emotions got riled.

"Ha! You joined the army so you could blow things

up." Chose the military and their secret missions over her. It still burned.

"So what if I did. You didn't have to dump me."

"What else could I do when you signed up without even talking to me about it first?"

"You would have said no."

"Of course, I would have. You know how I feel about violence." The world would be a better place if people would keep their hands and bullets to themselves.

"I didn't have a choice." He'd said it then and repeated it now.

"You made your choice," was her soft reply.

"I know, and I've regretted it more than you could ever imagine."

"So you're here to apologize?" She arched a brow. "Accepted. Have a good life."

"That's only half of the reason. I need your help."

She shook her head. "No."

"Come on, Maze. Why not?"

She couldn't admit that seeing him again roused all kinds of feelings she'd thought long buried. "Help you how? And why not ask your family to help you?" The Joneses were known to be connected.

"I can't ask them because they'll feel sorry for me. And then I'll have to hit them, and Da will get angry, and then there will be some yelling." His lips turned down. "Part of the reason Mum left was because we were so loud you know."

The vulnerable admission was so unlike Jakob she blurted out, "Bullshit. Who told you that?"

"She did, right before she had her people sedate me."

Maisy blinked. "Wait, what? When did this happen?"

"A few months ago. She kidnapped me and did some-

35

thing to me. My family says I was missing for more than three months. When I got back, I couldn't shift."

"But you just said you're a panda."

"A recent change. The first time it happened, I was minding my business, eating some bamboo—"

"Eating what?"

"Bamboo. Delicious. But not the point. My apartment was attacked."

"Holy hacking hairball. That was you in the news clips?" She gaped at him as the dots connected.

He nodded.

She paced. "Oh, Jakob. This is bad. So bad. You're in so much trouble. The Council—"

"Will want me arrested. I know. And maybe it's for the best. They need to see what my mother is capable of so they can stop her!"

She paused her steps and faced him. "I'll need to send them a report. You have to tell me everything you can."

"I told you, I don't remember what she did."

"I mean tell me everything about how you feel. The changes you've experienced since your return. Every little detail. It could be important." If his mother truly could make a shifter swap species, this was grave news. They had to find a way to stop it. "You said the change didn't hurt?"

"Not that I noticed. I mean I was feeling kind of itchy and caught my first flu a few weeks ago. I don't know how the humans do it. All that coughing and snot." He shuddered.

"And you ran a fever?" She grabbed a pad of paper and took notes.

"Hot and cold at the same time. Sweated my rump off.

Gained a ton of weight, too. Look at me. I'm fat." He poked his belly.

"Only because you haven't been working out, I'll bet."

"Because I'm depressed," he admitted with his lips turned down.

He looked cute. Too cute. She wanted to run her claws down that skin until he yodeled her name. Then she'd ribbon him for being a jerk. "Is it me, or are you taller? Stand up."

He definitely towered more than before, and she had to crane to see his face. He looked so upset. She wanted to grab those cheeks and kiss him and tell him she'd make it all better.

She retreated instead. "How much do you weigh?"

"Too much. More than you'd think for my size. Let me show you. Where's your scale?" He knew where to find it, under the workbench on the wall, the one that held all the tools of her trade, from mortar and pestle for grinding to Bunsen burner for blending at high heat.

She pointed, and Jakob slid out the scale. He stood on it. Like the couch, it creaked in protest and the dial ran out of space a second before the spring on it snapped. Given the scale went to three hundred pounds that was interesting.

She frowned. "You have packed on a few pounds, but that doesn't make you a panda. Pandas are small bears." Or at least the ones she'd cared for tended to be on the smaller size. The one on the television had been deemed oversized, hence the reason why many believed it was a hoax.

"I wish I could show you."

"Why can't you show me?"

"Because it doesn't come out on demand," he grumbled. "Trust me, I've been trying to get it to come out, but the first time it took my butt getting tranked before it took over. But that's not the worst of it."

"How can it be worse?" She really had to wonder.

"Because the damned thing can't throw a decent punch."

JAKOB GASPED as Maize slugged him in the gut. She'd always had a most excellent left hook.

"Wha— dat for?" he managed to sputter as he tried to breathe.

"Because you're an idiot. I can't believe you think the fact a panda can't throw a punch is the worst part of your situation."

"Wait, does this mean you believe me?"

She scowled, looking more gorgeous than he recalled. Her skin was smooth, her eyes bright and framed in dark lashes. Her kinky hair begged to be stroked.

While he didn't regret many things in life, signing up to become an elite soldier was one of them. He'd wanted to tell her the truth back then, that he had no choice. It was part of the deal his family made to keep Uncle Kevyn out of prison. At the time, he'd promised to keep his mouth shut. Despite not being able to tell her the entire truth, he'd hoped she'd understand. That she'd wait for him.

The deal was the Joneses would form an elite squad for a few years to pay off the family's debt—because if one

Jones fucked up, they all paid—but after she left, he had no reason to quit, so he and his brothers kept going on missions. The most dangerous ones usually, although they'd gotten choosier in the last few years. Some of his brothers even retired from the mercenary game. Jakob had thought himself about hanging up his combat boots and seeing if he could rekindle things with Maze.

Looking at the scowl on her lips and the fire in her eyes, he realized he might have waited too long.

"I'm sorry for how I handled things." He scrubbed at his face, feeling the bristles and lines of fatigue. "Would it help if I said I didn't want to leave?"

"No. And it doesn't matter. I got over you."

Jealousy reared its ugly head, and for a minute, he could feel the beast prickling, reacting to his emotions.

She tapped his nose. "Don't you dare shift inside."

He blinked. "Ow?"

"Don't be a baby roo about it."

"I wish I could be a roo," was his grumpy exclamation.

"Is it so bad that you're a bear? Pandas are considered to be highly prized given their rarity."

"I don't want to be a panda. I want to go back to being me!"

"We don't always get what we want," was her soft reply as she turned from him.

He reached out, only to let his hand drop. He'd lost the right to touch her a long time ago. "Can you help me?" he asked instead.

"Doubtful."

"Surely there's something we can try. Some ancient ritual. I'll do anything."

"I want to help you, but I've never even heard of such a thing."

"Would your grandpa maybe know?" As a tribal elder, he had access to ancient legends.

"I'll ask him in the morning. For now, get some sleep." When he eyed the main bedroom door—the room they'd shared for a time—she cleared her throat. "You get the couch or the second bedroom. But I warn you, it's messy. Peach isn't very tidy."

Who was Peach? His nose twitched, but the herbs she had hanging from the rafters, drying, made it impossible to filter the scents.

"I'll take the couch, if that's okay." He wanted to be by the door just in case he'd been followed.

"It's your back," was her flippant reply.

"Thanks, Maze. I appreciate you not turning me away." He'd been worried she'd slam the door in his face.

"You knew I wouldn't," she accused as she pulled out an extra blanket and tossed the bundle at him.

He'd counted on her ethics when it came to those in need. Funny how hers was the first face and name that came to mind when in desperation he'd sought someone who could aid him.

"I'd hoped you wouldn't," he replied. "But would have understood."

"I don't like trouble." She crossed her arms. "According to the news, the authorities are looking for you. Why?"

He shrugged. "Don't know for sure. They came pounding on my door. They never said why, and I wasn't about to go with them to find out. I can only assume it has to do with the bar burning down."

"Where's Anvil? No one has seen him since the fire."

It didn't surprise Jakob that she knew the bartender. After all, when they dated, they used to visit the tavern regularly. He could still picture Maze dancing, head tilted back, feet bare, arms and torso shimmying.

"I haven't seen Anvil since that night. I can only assume my mother still has him."

"Do you think he's still alive?" She gnawed her lower lip.

"I would imagine he is if he survived her treatment."

Her mouth turned down. "I can't believe what your mother did."

Was there anyone who didn't know of her perfidy? "Did you know she wants to rule the world?"

"Is she bonkers? That will never happen."

He shrugged. "I know that, and you know that, but Veronica is thinking on a whole different level than the rest of us."

"I can't believe she's alive. I can't imagine any way I'd ever leave my child."

"Yeah, well, can't really blame her. Kids are a handful. Messy. Loud. Right little shits at times, always breaking stuff and yelling."

Maze stared at him. "You don't really believe that, do you?"

"Like you said, why else would anyone leave their kid unless they're the worst brats ever?"

"Oh, Jakob." She sighed his name.

He didn't want pity. "Doesn't really matter. And the good news is I won't pass on whatever evil gene she owns since I doubt I'll ever be a dad."

"Why not? And don't say because you're a panda. You appear hale of body."

"Tell that to my head."

"Your mind has always been iffy," she teased with a twist of her hand, which almost brought a smile.

"There's not much future in what I have planned."

"Dare I ask what that is?"

"I am going to take down my evil mother's empire."

She eyed him. Arched a single brow. "Alone? I don't need to tell you that's suicidal and stupid. Obviously, you're determined to be some martyr because you have mommy issues."

"I don't want to die, but it will probably happen," he argued. "She's better armed than me."

"Then bring backup. Why would you even contemplate doing this alone?" She rolled her eyes, as expressive as ever. "You have family. Friends. Resources. Don't you want to succeed?"

"Yes. But—"

"But what? Call them."

"I can't."

"Why?"

"Because."

"Because why?"

He clamped his jaw tight rather than spew the jumbled emotions clogging him.

Maze pinpointed the problem. "You're afraid."

"Am not. Would I be going after my mother alone if I was scared?"

"Pshaw. I mean you're scared of your family. That the fact you're different will change how they feel about you."

"I don't need their pity."

"Do you really think they'll give a rat's ass that you're a panda rather than a roo?"

"I won't be one of them anymore."

"And? Let me ask you, how many sisters-in-law do you have?"

"A few."

"Are they family?"

"'Course they are." He saw where she was going but countered, "My situation is different."

"Why? Because you're feeling sorry for yourself?"

"You don't understand. I—"

She cuffed him hard, and his head snapped.

"Ow!" he yelped.

"Oh, so you can feel something other than pity. Wake up. The Jakob I used to know wasn't a fatalistic wuss."

He glared. "That Jakob is gone."

"No, he's being a whiny bitch." Maze stated as if it were fact.

"I am not a wuss."

"Then what are you?" she huffed, leaning close. "Because everyone knows the Joneses always stand together, and when they do…"

"They're unstoppable." He sighed. "I hate it when you make sense."

"Probably a good thing we never got married then," she muttered. "Night, Jakob."

She thrust a pillow at him and left the room, but her stinging words lingered.

She'd forced him to look within. See what an idiot he was being. Why would he cut off his nose to spite his face? She was right. It was suicidal to go alone. And yes, it would be hard to tell his family what had happened to him, but deep down, he knew they'd love him no matter what.

He'd call them in the morning. First, he needed some sleep.

The couch groaned ominously as he lay upon it, barely fitting, his body curved since he was too long. His belly grumbled, protesting the lack of bamboo, which probably explained his nightmares. In the morning, he'd have to talk to Maze about getting a stash.

Maze. Just thinking of her made him relax. As beautiful as ever. Fierce, too. How he wished things could have been different. If only he could have told her the truth back then. She would have never divulged his family secret.

Instead, he'd lost her. The one woman he'd loved, the only mate for him, and he'd screwed up. He'd be alone forever. All alone.

The tiny violin brought a frown. Was he truly going to give in that easily? Maze was worth fighting for. What they used to have had been so beautiful. How could he not even try to give it a chance? Sure, she was mad now, but she had a right to her anger. He would apologize, properly this time, and finally explain the reasons behind his departure, ask for forgiveness, earn it. Seduce her...

Mmm. He fell asleep on that thought and woke to a tiger cub snarling in his face!

MAISY WALKED out of her bedroom just as Peach leaped onto Jakob's chest. The tiger cub snarled and startled him awake.

Not a good idea in his condition. His eyes widened, his mouth opened, his body tensed, and she feared what might happen.

She flung herself at Jakob and the snarling striped bundle of fur, shouting, "Don't you dare hurt my daughter!"

A daughter who was home early from a walkabout with her grandfather, and what a surprise, she'd decided to sneak in. Nothing Peach liked more than making her mother scream and drop things. Then the brat would giggle. A good thing she was cute or else…

Jakob stared at Peach, who remained perched on his chest, and said in a very tight voice, "You have a kid."

"Yes."

No need to say she wasn't his. He would have smelled it. She also saw no need to mention the fact that Peach was actually a foundling. She'd come across the feral child in the outback when she was about two. She could only imagine what might have happened to her biological mother.

Maisy scooped Peach into her arms and snuggled the furry head. Scientists could say what they wanted. Some tiger cubs did purr. She held on tight as the child switched into her gangly limbs, and adorably exclaimed, "Mama, I'm home."

"Indeed, you are, my fuzzy girl." She nuzzled Peach's cheek. "Where is your pappy?"

"I lost him," Peach exclaimed with a vigorous bounce.

"Again?" Maisy exclaimed.

Her daughter liked to play a game of evade the adults. She had an uncanny ability to disappear and only be found when she wanted to. The first time she'd escaped her bedroom, Maisy had been sure a dingo stole her. "Poor pappy. He's going to be worried."

"Pappy knows I'm here. I waved to him before I went inside."

Maisy sighed. "Why didn't he come in? What did you hooligans do this time?" Because the only time her father didn't pop in to say hello was when he knew Maisy would give him heck for teaching her kid yet another thing she was too young to know. Lessons she remembered having as a child. Never mind she'd turned out okay. This was her kid.

Her daughter tried to adopt an innocent face. "We didn't do nuthin'. We was good."

"I highly doubt that," Maisy grumbled, doing her best to not look at a shell-shocked Jakob. Surely, he'd known she had a kid. It wasn't as if she'd kept it secret in the two years since she'd adopted her. Then again, her only contact in the years since they split was the occasional run-in with one of his brothers. Why she'd seen Jax not that long ago with Mari, a hybrid human, in tow.

"You got married?" he asked as he sat up, his expression sad.

Why would he be sad? He'd made it obvious he never wanted to be tied down. Look at him, single all the years since their split. Never mind she was single, too. She had a rambunctious reason to be cautious.

"Just because I have a kid doesn't mean I'm married, and it's pretty patriarchal of you to think so," Maisy declared.

"That's not what I meant. That is…I…uh," he stammered.

He was saved from replying and thrown to the tigers as Peach pointed to him and said, "Who is that?"

Peach was used to seeing patients coming and going. What she didn't usually do was pounce them.

"My name is Jakob. I'm an old friend of your mother's."

"Mama has no friends." Said with all the honesty of a child who saw too much.

"I do too have friends," Maisy hotly declared. "I just don't see them often."

"I'm sure your mother is very busy," Jakob replied. "I don't have many friends either. Mostly just my brothers and uncles."

"I don't have a brother. Or a sister," Peach solemnly declared. "Mama won't make one."

Heat filled Maisy's cheeks as her daughter kept revealing intimate things that had Jakob leaning forward and saying, "You need someone special to make babies with."

Peach nodded solemnly. "I asked Pappy to make one

with mama because he's special, but he said no." Her lips turned down.

"With good reason," a startled Jakob exclaimed.

Given the way Peach eyed him up and down, Maisy could almost predict what she'd ask next.

"Is anyone hungry? I know I'm hungry. Breakfast?" Maisy asked much too brightly.

"I don't suppose I could shower first?" Jakob asked.

"You stink," Peach declared with a wrinkle of her nose.

"Peach Daisy Williams!" Maisy exclaimed. "That was rude. Apologize at once."

A lower lip jutted as Peach muttered, "Sorry."

Jakob chuckled. "Don't give the girl crap. She is right. Given I've been on the lam for a while with no access to a proper shower, I can't imagine I smell good."

Maisy wouldn't know. Her sense of smell was actually worse than a human's.

Peach squirmed out of her grip and moved to stand in front of Jakob. "I know you. I seen your picture."

"On the television?" Jakob queried. "I hear I made the news."

Peach shook her head. "Mommy keeps your picture hidden in her undies drawer."

Oh no she didn't. Maisy really wished taping her daughter's mouth shut wasn't considered a crime. At this rate, Jakob would know everything about her—all the embarrassing bits—before lunch.

She had to stop this. She had to— She tuned in to what he told Peach.

"You wanna hear something funny, fluffs?" Jakob drawled. "I have your mom's picture in my wallet. Or I did. Not sure if it survived the raid on my place."

Maisy wanted to ask why he carried around her

picture. It had been years since they'd been together. However, her daughter wasn't done interrogating him yet.

"Why are you sleeping on the couch?"

"I'm sick."

Peach cocked her head. "You don't look sick."

"My illness is inside," he admitted, putting a hand to his chest.

"When I hurt inside, I cry. Then mama gets me ice cream."

His lips twitched. "I don't cry, but when I'm feeling blue, I'm an ice cream kind of guy, too."

"What flavor?" she asked as if it were the most important thing in the world.

"There is only one true flavor," he declared. And then as if choreographed, they both said, "Chocolate." Then burst into laughter.

Her daughter giggled with her ex-lover. It was the most amazing thing ever. The most dangerous, too. She couldn't let herself fall for him again.

Nor could she let Peach.

"We should leave Jakob alone. He just woke up."

"I'm fine," he said, casting a quick glance at her before turning back to Peach. "How old are you?"

Peach held up four fingers.

"Wow. You're older than me, then. Your mother says I'm worse than a toddler."

That brought a little girl snort of, "You're old."

He grimaced. "I know. And fat."

"You need to exercise." Spoken with all the head-bobbing wisdom a child could manage.

"I'll admit, I've been a bit lazy lately, but that's all about to change."

"Speaking of change"—Maisy clapped her hands

—"Jakob needs a shower, and you need to find a brush so I can do something for your hair." It spread out in a halo around Peach's head. Super cute, but impractical when it came to chores.

"But, Mama, I am not done talking to Jakob."

"Room. Brush. Now. When you're both tidied up, you can chat some more."

"Fine," Peach grumbled, dragging her feet.

She went into the bedroom cluttered with toys and other things a growing girl needed. The house itself was an okay size for their needs, but Maisy had been thinking of moving. The thought of leaving the only home she'd known for so long was daunting; however, unless she was planning to homeschool, soon Peach would need to enroll. Since she wasn't close enough to a bus route, either they had to drive a fair distance each day or move.

Jakob waited until Peach had closed the door before softly asking, "Who's her father?"

"No one you know."

And not a factor, given Peach was orphaned. Maisy never did find out who her parents were. Never heard of any missing person reports. No story about a couple and their child going missing, as if Peach's parents never existed. But then where had Peach come from?

Maisy hadn't cared when she brought her home. Finding the baby girl seemed a stroke of providence. What were the chances a feline shifter would find a cub? Who knew having a daughter would finally fill most of the hole left inside her when she and Jakob split up? Sleeping with a few different guys hadn't managed to make her forget Jakob, but having a little person relying on her did help fill in the previously empty times when she would have moped.

"Your daughter is cute. Like her mother."

"She's also too bright and curious by far."

A result of spending too much time with adults instead of kids. Another thing to feel guilty about. The only time Peach saw other kids was when Maisy did the long trek into the city and brought her to play places. Apart from that, she spent time with Maisy's father, who took to being a grandfather like a croc to water.

Herbert Williams spent every weekend with the kid, and just this past month, they'd gone on a pilgrimage together into the wild. Two weeks without a cub snuggling up in the middle of the night. Fourteen long days where she cooked for one person and didn't wipe up sticky spots.

"Sounds like she takes after her mother."

Another compliment that she ignored.

"Why did you lie about having my picture?" Surely it wasn't true.

"What makes you think I did?"

"Because we broke up a long time ago, Jakob, and we're not getting back together."

He opened his mouth as if to say something, and then his shoulders dropped. "I know. But that doesn't mean I ever gave up hope that one day you'd forgive me."

Forgive him for breaking her heart? Never, because it would probably end up smashed to bits again.

"I forgive you. Happy?" she snapped.

"No." A stark and honest answer. "Do you only have the one kid? I always pictured you with a bushel of babies."

She arched a brow. "A bushel? That's a lot of babies."

He grinned. "My da always said you could never have too many." His lips turned down as he added, "My mum didn't agree."

This vulnerable side of him was new. "She must have at one time, given she had you and your brothers."

"And I have a half-sister, too. I don't know who her da is. I've never met her or my half-brother. But I saw them on television."

"Why not try and find her?"

He snorted. "I've been trying, but Mum didn't stay missing this long because she was careless."

"You've been looking for her?"

"Since we found out she's alive."

"What about your father? How's he handling it?" she asked.

His lips pressed into a line. "Da won't talk about it."

"Can't say as I blame him. Relationships are tricky things at the best of times." She turned from him.

"Are you seeing anyone?"

She stiffened. "That's none of your business."

"It is if I'm going to court you."

"Court me?" She snorted as she whirled to gape at him. "I just said we weren't getting back together." Tell that to her racing heart.

"Yet," he countered. "But that's because you're confusing me with old Jakob. New Jakob is not a jerk."

"Not interested."

"Give it a chance."

"No. You and I will never be together," she huffed.

Hopefully he couldn't smell the lie.

6

JAKOB HAD THROWN Maze off balance. He could see it. Only fair given the loop she'd thrown him.

She had a kid.

With someone else.

It hurt. More than he could have said. Seeing the bright-eyed tyke was a reminder that, had they stayed together, they'd have had a few cubs of their own. Instead, she'd moved on without him.

The good news was Daddy didn't appear to be in the picture. Which meant there was room for him to prove himself, but only after he solved his panda dilemma. After his epiphany of the previous night, he was eager to call his family, only he had no phone.

"Hey, Maze," he shouted. "You got a phone hiding somewhere?"

"You can borrow my cell." Her bedroom door opened, and he caught the flying mobile.

It took him but a moment to dial.

The house line answered with a friendly, "Hey, Maisy.

How's it going? Did you get that box of supplies I sent you? Did Peach like her present?"

"You knew Maisy had a daughter?" Jakob said softly. He didn't need to announce himself.

Jaycon immediately knew who was on the other end of the line. "Hey, bro. Er, how's it going?"

"You tell me. Apparently, you know more than I do. Why didn't you tell me Maisy had a kid?"

"Didn't know you'd be interested."

"You should have told me."

"You were broken up. I didn't think you cared."

"You thought wrong," he growled.

"Yeah, so, um, good thing you called. The whole family's been going crazy since the shitshow they've been playing on the news."

The reminder brought a groan, and Jakob looked at the thatched roof of the hut. "Is there anyone who hasn't seen that footage?"

"No. What were you thinking, harboring a bear in the city?" Jaycon chided. "You should have called. If you needed to stash someone, we would have helped you." His brother assumed the bear was someone else.

His family didn't know his shameful secret, and rather than tell, he lied. "I was doing a friend a favor. Kind of backfired. And now I'm a wanted man. How bad is the jail time for smuggling exotic pets?"

"I'd worry less about that and more about the other pending charges."

"What charges?"

"Anvil is back."

The statement threw Jakob for a loop. "What? When?"

"The day the cops raided your place. Rumor has it,

Anvil went into a police station and told them that he went into hiding because he was scared of you. That you torched his bar and threatened to kill him if he said anything."

"That's a load of dingo shit."

"Obviously, but the humans believed him. And you didn't help matters by letting that idiot bear rush out in a panic."

"He just wanted to escape," Jakob muttered. Instead, he'd made his situation worse.

"I assume, given the phone number you're calling from, that you're with Maisy?"

"As if you didn't know." All the Joneses wore trackers now since the kidnappings. The family was determined to not be caught unaware again.

"Your device is malfunctioning, again. We couldn't get a proper bead on your signal." Because he'd dug it out and dropped it down a sewer.

"Yeah, I'm at Maze's for the moment." He paced. "But if the cops are looking for me, I probably shouldn't stay."

"You're probably okay sitting tight there for a little while. I doubt they'll make the connection. It's been ages since you dated."

It had been, yet at times, the memory of their time together proved so vivid it felt like yesterday. Especially now that she was within reach and yet even further away than ever.

He rubbed his temple. "Is Da around?"

"He's out with Uncle Kyle making some final preparations."

"Tell him I'm okay. No need to send out the troops."

"I told him you were okay the second you called. They're now prepping for Plan B."

"What's Plan B?" Jakob asked.

"Taking down the mothership. We got a clue on Mum's whereabouts, but Da was holding off until we knew for sure where you were. Now that you're out of the way, the plan is to roll out, infiltrate her hideaway, and take her into custody."

"You have an address for Mum?" Jakob brightened. Perhaps she had a way to reverse what she'd done. "Where is she? When do we leave?" To think he'd planned to do this alone. He should have trusted his family.

"Um. Er. Ah," Jaycon stammered, and Jakob frowned as he shifted the phone to his other ear.

"Why are you stammering? Spit it out."

"You can't come."

"Says who?"

"Says me. Think about it. You're a known and wanted man. We just need one person getting a peek at you and any covert operation we undertake will be in the toilet."

The logic snapped his mouth shut for a second. "I could wear a disguise."

"You need to sit this one out, brother. Work on clearing your name. Uncle Klaus is working on a plan of defense, so the sooner you get home, the sooner you can fight the charges and prove Anvil is lying."

"I'm not going home and playing nice with the courts." He couldn't afford to waste time with bureaucracy.

"You can't stay with Maisy forever. If the cops find out…"

No need to finish that sentence. Jakob glanced at her closed door. "I'll leave today."

"Good."

"Not going to ask me where I'm going?"

Jaycon snorted. "As if you'd tell me the truth. Just be sure to check in so Da doesn't lose his shit again."

"Will do." He hung up, suddenly tired. He wanted to nap again, sleep until his world went back to normal. Only he couldn't sleep, mostly because he had an itch.

Lumbering to his feet, he raised his arms into a deep stretch. For a moment, with his head back and eyes closed, he was vulnerable.

She attacked. The pounce allowed her to attach herself to him with her sharp little claws like Velcro, but even more secure. He knew better than to panic, but he was a little anxious. In his family, the babies were only just starting, and he usually stayed clear. Add to that he only had experience with boys. No young girls.

He shouldn't yell. He might scare her.

He shouldn't make a sudden movement for the same reason.

He stood still, and she took that as an invitation to dig deeper and climb his leg.

He might have let out an unmanly, "Eep."

Maisy stuck her head out the door and barked, "Get down right this instant and put some clothes on, Peach Daisy Williams, or so help me…"

The threat hung in the air, but it worked. The cub dropped to the floor and, shooting a reproachful look at her mother, headed back to her room.

"Thanks," he said.

"I don't know what got into her," Maisy muttered as she entered the living room fully dressed. "She doesn't usually attack people."

"I wasn't attacking him," huffed the little girl as she emerged from her room, having donned a romper. "I was saying good morning."

"Most people say good morning with words," Maisy declared, shaking a finger at her daughter.

"I was going to once I climbed him." The tyke grinned, and Maisy sighed.

"What have I said about showing strangers your tiger?"

"But he's not a stranger."

The banter between child and mother proved fascinating. Jakob soaked it in, amazed it hadn't devolved into a wrestling match yet.

"No climbing guests!"

"Fine," Peach huffed. She approached, stopping before him, head tilted before extending her arms.

"Um." He stood, unsure of his next move.

"Pick me up," demanded the imperious cub.

"Manners!" barked Maisy.

"Please." The girl batted her lashes, and he found himself scooping the child, holding her at arm's length.

Maisy snorted. "Good grief, she's not contagious. Stick her on your hip."

A good thing Peach understood what that meant because it wouldn't have occurred to him. But the child knew how to hold on and then peeked at him with the biggest brown eyes ever.

"Hi," she said.

"Hey."

"You're tall."

"Um, thanks?"

She patted his cheeks. "Teddy bear."

How did she know? "Can you smell me?"

"I seen it."

She must mean the television broadcast. "I'm supposed to be a roo," he confided.

"Not anymore." Said with the bluntness of youth.

Maisy heard. "Peach. That's not nice. Jakob is very sad."

"Not anymore." Again, Peach patted his cheeks.

Perceptive child. He actually didn't feel all that bummed at the moment.

Peach stiffened in his grip and cocked her head, her eyes taking on a dreamy cast before she murmured, "The weird smelly, bad men are coming."

"What?" He blinked at her strange choice of words. "You mean the garbage guys?" He would have thought Maze was too far from the city for those kinds of services.

"*Bad.* Men. With guns." The little girl looked past him to the front door.

"Um, Maze," he called out. "Is your child some kind of fortune teller?"

Turning from the kitchen counter, Maize took in her daughter, then his face, then the pointed finger, and cursed. "How many and how long?"

Peach shrugged. "Soon."

"Meaning we don't have time to take my Range Rover." Maisy cursed in a way that sounded delightfully dirty coming from her luscious lips.

But it was the reason that had him turning to stone. "Wait, are we about to be attacked?"

"You idiot. You were followed," she snapped as she dragged out a pair of backpacks from under the sink.

"Are those bug-out bags?" he asked.

"Ever since your mother ratted our kind out, I've been worried about someone coming after me and Peach."

His mother and her diabolical schemes. He eyed Maze and hardened his jaw. "Take the girl and go. I'll distract them."

Maze snorted. "You idiot. No one is staying behind."

She thrust a pack at him before throwing on her own. Peach had a smaller version already on her back.

Peach grinned at them. "Are we playing hide and seek?"

"Yes," Maze said. "To win, the only person who is allowed to find you is me, Jakob, or Pappy. Don't talk to strangers. Don't be followed. And most of all, don't get caught, or you won't get any ice cream."

"Two scoops?" Peach bargained.

"Three with a cherry if you make it to Pappy before I do."

In a wink, the child had dropped through a hatch in the floor.

"Aren't we following?" he asked as Maze hinged the trapdoor shut and then slid the rug back over it.

"In a minute. First, we should see who's coming after us. Could be we're panicking for nothing."

To think he was supposed to be the professional mercenary. "Um, yeah. I don't suppose you have a gun?" Judging by the cool look on her face, he was going to say that was a no.

"You know how I feel about firearms."

He did. Yet another reason he couldn't tell her of his choice all those years ago. "Exactly how do you expect us to greet them then?"

"With a smile." She dropped her bag onto the floor and headed for the door. Before he could stop her, she'd stepped outside and said, "Hello. Can I help you?"

MAISY FIGURED she probably seemed really brave stepping out of her hut instead of racing down into the crawlspace and using it to conceal her escape. However, it was more important she give Peach a head start. A decision reinforced when she saw who—or should she say what—they faced.

Four people in suits and shades emerged from a large SUV with tinted windows. Not worrisome in and of itself, except for the guns in the hands of three of them. They could have stepped off the stage of a *Men in Black* movie, their ensembles identical except for the one female in the group. She wore a skirt instead of slacks.

"Are you Ms. Williams?" asked the skinniest fellow, his human scent not hinting one bit at fear. Then again, why would he be scared of little ol' Maisy?

"I am. Who are you?" Because they had no identifying emblems or uniforms.

"You can call me Agent Loomer. These are my associates, Jugger, Kline, and Pumpernickel." He waved a hand.

Loomer didn't name the agency he worked for. Oversight? Or because it wasn't one recognized by the government or law? "What can I help you with?"

"We're seeking a fugitive. Name of Jakob Jones."

She spat on the ground. "That good for nothing. What's he done now?"

"Have you seen him?" asked Loomer.

"Not since I dumped his ass. Why? Is he in trouble?" She hoped Jakob had the sense to remain out of sight inside.

"Mr. Jones is wanted for questioning. He is considered dangerous."

"Really?" she drawled. "I find that hard to believe. He's always been a bit of a teddy bear."

"Interesting that you mention bear, ma'am. Do you have any knowledge about panda bears? Perhaps the whereabouts of a missing one?"

"You still looking for it? I saw the panda escape on the news. Do you think Jakob smuggled it into the country?" She shook her head. "Can't say as I'm surprised he turned to a life of crime."

She could see the fellow getting frustrated, and yet each moment they spent talking was a minute her daughter was using to get away.

Or not.

Her blood ran cold as she heard a tiny growl. A glance over her shoulder showed a striped tiger cub standing at the corner of the house, hackles up, looking to protect her mama.

"Well, well, what do we have here? More exotic animals." Those shades gave no hint of Loomer's expression. "It seems a rather large coincidence, don't you think, Agent Kline?"

"I think she's his accomplice," said the female of the group, her tone flat.

This conversation was rapidly going downhill. "This isn't what it seems. I'm a vet. I fix animals. This one is a patient who must have gotten free." She reached down and grabbed her cub by the scruff of the neck as she went to streak past. "If you give me a second, I'll put her back in her cage. The barn is right over there." She pointed to a building where she did most of her vet work.

"Keep your hands where we can see them!" Another of the guys in shades raised his weapon as he barked.

"I'm unarmed," she shouted. In that moment, a thousand possibilities ran through her mind, all of them involving shifting into her panther, which was a no-no in front of the humans. Bad enough Peach had transformed and shown herself.

But how to get out of the situation? She couldn't be arrested. They'd take Peach from her and put her in a real cage.

She backed away, Peach tucked to her chest, as the voices kept making demands to put down the cub and hold up her hands. Her heart raced as she looked desperately for a way to protect her child.

Jakob chose that moment to burst out of the cottage. It was less a calculated rush and more a clumsy stumble that sent him from two teetering panda legs into a tucked furry ball that startled the humans enough he managed to bowl a pair over. Before they could rise, he was trying to stand and wavering on his feet, swinging around giant paws that looked fearsome but did nothing.

The agents didn't panic like normal humans would when faced with a bear. At a signal from Loomer, Jugger aimed his weapon.

Thwick. The dart hit the big bear in the shoulder. It didn't slow him one bit as he fell against the agent, who suddenly wasn't a human anymore but a rhino shredding her clothes.

How was that possible? She'd never even scented it. None of them presented as skinwalkers, and yet, in a moment, three of the four had shifted while Loomer—still in his suit—took careful aim, ready to shoot the panda again.

Peach snarled and wiggled hard enough that Maisy lost her grip on her daughter. The cub hit the ground on four paws, and Maisy could only watch in bemused horror as her kid threw herself into the fray. The good news was no one was trying to hurt Peach. They appeared to be trying to subdue Jakob, who struggled in his bear shape. Enough was enough. She pulled a long wooden tube from her pocket and put it to her lips.

Thunk. The dart hit flesh, and the female rhino dropped to the ground.

Pfft. The second shifter, Pumpernickel, with his blunt tusks, snorted before toppling. Loomer had climbed onto the hood of the SUV, avoiding sharp cub teeth, while Kline, the gorilla, grappled with a panda in a battle to see who would hug the tightest. It didn't look like he'd win that contest.

As a bear, Jakob lacked the grace she recalled when he was a roo. No wonder he felt ill at ease in his skin.

Pfft. Pfft.

Only when all four of the agents slept on the ground did Maisy sigh. What a mess.

"Peach, call your pappy. Tell him to meet us at the woohoo tree."

"Rawr." The cub raced past her for the cottage and the phone.

"Woowoo what?" Jakob asked, his shift sudden enough she got an eyeful of male flesh before averting her gaze.

Rather than reply to his question, she wagged a finger. "You! This is your fault."

"I don't know how they found me."

"Doesn't matter. Given they've obviously got us associated, I'll have to leave." She gazed upon her cottage. Her home for the last decade. No longer a safe place.

"I'm sorry, Maze. I never meant to bring trouble." He hung his head.

She didn't need to see his expression to know he was sincerely contrite. "You fight like shit."

"I know. I need to find my mother so she can change me back."

"If it's even possible." She shook her head. "You gotta be ready to accept the possibility this is permanent."

"I don't like it." His lower lip almost jutted.

"Then fix it."

"How? You just said I might be stuck like this forever."

"If that's the case, then you need to learn how to use your new body."

"Easier said than done. Know any pandas who can teach me?"

Peach emerged, a little girl once more, wearing her backpack. "Pappy says last one there is a smelly cat." She bounced, eager to go.

"Then you'd better get moving."

Peach hesitated. "Are you coming?"

"Just let me grab my bag." As Peach bolted off, leaving the cleared yard to enter the brush, Maisy turned on Jakob. "Give me a hand with the bodies."

"Gotta knife? I can make it quick."

She blinked. "Not to kill them idiot. I have cages we can lock them in to give us extra time. Get dressed first, then give me a hand." Because he was hella distracting.

While he ran inside for his clothes, she hit the barn, sliding open the doors and readying four cages. She currently had no wild creatures recovering, a rarity in her occupation where everyone for miles around with a hurt animal came to see her, including cryptids.

About to head back to the bodies, Jakob arrived, dragging the first one, the rhino fellow, with his gray leathery skin and sharp tusk. Jakob heaved him into a cage and waved her off when she would have gone to help. "Just make sure he stays locked up. We don't need them on our tail."

She didn't just secure the cage. She also ensured she got a blood sample from the rhino. In his animal shape, he smelled as expected, and yet the bundle of clothes, ragged shreds for the most part, that Jakob dumped inside the barn all oozed of human. A dichotomy she'd like to study, but it would have to wait. They'd wasted too much time.

Once all the agents were locked up, she slid the barn door shut and returned to her house to grab a few extra things, including her pack. Jakob hadn't said much, and when he did, it wasn't with the brashness she'd expected.

"I'm sorry I led them here."

"Too late for that now. What's done is done."

"I won't bother you again," he said, turning to leave.

She should let him go. "Wait. Where are you going?"

He shrugged. "I'll figure something out."

On an impulse, she said, "You're coming with me."

"I can't. I'm a wanted man."

"Maybe you are, and yet those weren't cops."

"They called themselves agents."

"For what? I didn't find any identification in their clothes. And despite smelling human, they're skinwalkers like you and me."

"Do you think FUC sent them?"

"The Furry United Coalition agents I've met always identified themselves, and they have badges."

"If not FUC, then who sent them?" he asked, frowning.

"No idea. But we should take a quick peek to see if there's any clues before we take off."

She searched the ground for more shredded clothes, one hand on her blow pipe loaded with tranquilizer darts. Strong ones because she usually dealt with wounded animals and they could be unpredictable.

Jakob searched the SUV and emerged wearing pants he'd found but with his hands empty.

"Nothing?" she asked.

He shook his head. "Not even registration papers. You?"

"Nada. They came in clean, making it even more likely these fellows were up to no good." She frowned at them. "Who would be coming after you like that?"

He sounded so grim as he said, "My mum."

8

THERE WAS no one else with the kind of money needed to hire muscle interested in taking him alive.

Why did his mum want him again? Had she seen his footage on television? And why had she dumped him in the first place? Was it because she thought she'd failed?

Whatever the reason, he needed to get away from Maisy and Peach before he brought more trouble. He entered the cottage and retrieved the bug-out bag, handing Maze hers as she entered. "You find Peach, and I'll do my best to create a path that leads them away."

She snorted. "We saw how well that worked the first time."

He scrubbed a hand through his hair. "Yeah, well, guess I'll have to try harder."

"You won't get far if you can't fight. That was pathetic."

He grimaced. "I know. Damn new body doesn't work the way I expect it to."

"Until it does, you shouldn't be alone."

"I'll go see my family."

"Actually, I have a better idea. A place to keep you safe while teaching you how to be a proper panda," she stated.

"Where? The zoo? I don't see how spending time in a cage will help me. I'd be better off watching those *Kung Fu Panda* movies."

"Not a bad idea. Maybe we can rent it on the plane."

"Plane?" He blinked. "Are you insane? We can't get on a plane or anything that requires identification."

"You're assuming that we'll be using our current names. I'll have that taken care of when I arrange our flight."

"Are we going somewhere?"

"Yes. Back to school."

"Like fuck I am," he exhaled.

"Actually, more like FUCN'A, the Furry United Coalition Newbie Academy. It's in Canada."

He shook his head. "No way. No ARSHOL for me!" He'd heard of the place, the Animal Rescue Special House of Learning, started a few years ago after Mastermind's reign of terror. It provided a safe place where shifters not only learned the skills to combat future threats to their society but also helped those affected by Mastermind's experiments.

"I don't see what the problem is. You need to learn how to defend yourself. And you need to be safe while doing it. We both know the Academy is your safest bet."

"It's a whole continent away for starters."

"Even better. What are the chances your mother will come after us there?"

"Is it me, or did you say us?" He couldn't help but feel a spurt of excitement.

"Someone needs to make sure you get there in one piece, not to mention the whole human-scent-hiding-askinwalker ability needs to be further explored. I've got samples of the four fake agents, plus scraps of their clothes. FUCN'A has a fully equipped lab. Maybe we can get answers. Not just about the scent thing but your panda, too."

"What about Peach?"

Her lips turned down. "She'll be safe with her pappy while I'm gone."

"Or you could just give me the samples. I promise I'll get them to the lab."

She shook her head. "Peach will be fine without me for a few days. This is important. If someone has found a way to mask scent and change a person's animal genome, then we're all in trouble."

"You really think this is the best idea?"

"I don't think we really have a choice."

A heavy sigh left him. "If I'm going to back to school, then do me a favor?

"What?"

"I want a superhero lunch box."

She punched him in the arm.

"Ow!"

"Don't be such an idiot. This is serious."

She was right; it was serious, and scary. He'd never meant to draw Maisy into his problems, and now she wanted to help. It was more than he deserved. There wasn't much to say after they left her place, and not just because he was trying to not huff and puff as he followed the hard pace Maisy set. His mind still whirled.

Had his mother come after him? Why? He'd assumed she'd been the one to let him go. But what if that were a mistake? Perhaps he'd escaped or someone else had helped him.

The route they took meandered quite a bit, with Maisy backtracking in a few spots, covering their tracks. He trusted her and not just because she was his only choice. If anyone knew how to hide in the bush, it was this girl. Her father had taught her well, and once upon a time, when he was a roo, he would have been a match for her skills, but his heavy feet were noisy and clumsy. Maybe after some time spent at the Academy he would be light on his toes again.

It was nightfall before they approached a gnarly tree, wider than several people holding hands could hug, lit in ghostly moss that glowed as twilight gave way to night.

"Say hello to the woohoo tree," she stated.

"Why woohoo?"

"Climb inside the trunk and you'll see," was her cryptic reply. "Throw your pack in first, though."

He tossed his bag in and heard it hit something, followed by the slide of fabric. Next, he set his hands on the opening in the bole, putting one leg in at a time, feeling a firm surface. He crouched inside on a ledge, his bulk blocking all the outside light. Reaching in front of him, he felt nothing in his way. How big was the hollow?

He turned his head to ask over his shoulder, "Now what?"

Rather than reply, Maisy shoved him hard enough that he toppled onto his ass and plummeted downward. The ledge he'd been on was the top of a slide. He shot down. And down. The serpentine slide was steep and narrow, so he kept his arms over his chest and his legs tight together as he flew.

He could hear a feminine echo, "Woo! Hoo!" as Maze followed him down the unexpected chute. He had a moment at the bottom to realize he'd emerged into a cavern full of light, and then he was airborne.

"Argh!" He flew for a moment before hitting the water with a splash and sinking like a stone. Not far, thankfully. The moment he found the bottom he stood up, his head just emerging from the underground lake. And then he was back under as he failed to move out of the way and Maze hit him as she was ejected from the tube.

They stood together, her laughing, him glowering, mostly because she could have told him what to expect.

"Look who's a sour pussy," she said, tweaking his nose.

"I'm wet."

"But the good news is you don't stink as badly anymore." Her eyes sparkled with mirth.

Their gazes caught. Her laughter faded. They stared, their faces getting closer and closer—

"Mama! Teddy! I beat you."

The high-pitched voice severed the moment. Maze sloshed past him to the shore, a rocky lip rounded by time and water. He followed, glancing around him at the hanging stalactites, noting the clarity of the water. As for the light, it was provided by smokeless torches set around the lake. They illuminated enough to see the walls had been smoothed, all the better for the art etched and painted upon it.

Heaving himself out of the water, he noticed more signs of habitation, such the leather curtains hanging over cave entrances, one of which pulled aside to reveal a wiry man with tight iron-colored curls. Herbert Williams, Maisy's dad, appeared the same as Jakob recalled, if a tad more weathered. The guy spent his life outside, and apparently underground.

"What is this place?" Jakob asked as he pulled off his shirt and wrung it out. His bug-out bag sat on a nearby rock. He hoped the bag was waterproof.

"Not too sure. Some of the drawings appear to date back over ten thousand years, but at the same time, there are some advanced stone working techniques. You can see it in the furniture inside the caves, which places it more recently, perhaps the last few thousand years or so," Maisy informed him.

Both very old. "How did you find it?"

"Ancient family secret," was Herbert's squinty-eyed reply. "What's this I hear about men with guns coming after Peach?"

"Not Peach. Him." Maze jabbed a finger in his direction.

"And you brought him here?" Herbert sounded and looked less than impressed.

"No one followed me."

"Hmph." Clear disdainful disbelief. "Did you set the trap?"

"Of course." Maisy snorted. "No one is going to find your secret thrill ride."

"How long you planning to hide here?" Herbert asked. "I've got enough supplies for four for a week, but I can easily hunt for more."

"Jakob and I are only spending the night. I need to go somewhere with him."

"Can I come?" Peach bounced.

"Not this time. I won't be gone long."

The claim didn't matter. The little girl's lips turned down, and Jakob almost opened his mouth to say something that would cheer her. A look from Maze snapped his jaw shut.

"You have to protect Pappy from the bad guys," Maze stated, instead of giving in to the cutest face ever. Seriously, Jakob was fairly certain the child was part witch. She'd definitely bespelled him.

"I do?" the little girl breathed, her eyes wide. She wore a long T-shirt that went down to her knees, a cast-off of Maze's he'd wager, given it bore a faded Led Zeppelin logo.

"Pappy is getting old," Maze continued, ignoring her father's snort as he turned away lest his amusement give away the truth.

Jakob wandered closer to the old man and in a low hush said, "Any way you can tie Maze up and keep her here with you?"

Herbert cast him a sardonic gaze. "And die the moment she gets loose? You know she has a temper."

He did. He'd seen it on more than one occasion, over the top and extreme, like her decision to break up with him before he'd even left on his first mercenary tour.

Then refusing his calls.

"She's in danger if she sticks with me."

"She and that child are in danger every single day."

Being a shifter meant taking extra precautions, but Jakob had always accepted it as a fact of life. "Has she told you about my problem?"

"That you're an asshat who wouldn't know responsibility if it bit you in the ass?"

He blinked. "Uh, not that problem. And I had my reasons at the time. I was talking about the fact my roo is now a panda."

Herbert turned to stare at him. "Repeat that again. Slowly."

"My mother turned me into a panda."

"Did you hit your head on the slide?"

"He's telling the truth." Maze sidled close, Peach on her hip, sucking a thumb, her head tucked against her mother.

"He's a bear? But how?" Herbert eyed him more closely, his gaze tracking up and down. "His smell..."

"Is off, I know. I didn't notice before because of the reek of him. If I didn't know him better, I'd say he was—"

"Human!" Peach pointed.

Jakob grimaced. "Now that's not nice."

"How fascinating." Herbert leaned close and sniffed.

"The Council needs to know what's happened to him. What his mother is capable of."

"I don't want Teddy to go bye-bye." Peach reached for him. At a loss, he reached back, and she climbed into his arms and patted his cheeks. "I like your bear."

He gave Maze a panicked look before managing, "Your cat's pretty cool, too." The right answer apparently since the child beamed.

"Can you roll like Po?"

"Who?"

"Kung Fu Panda," Maze snickered. "I told you, you need to watch those movies."

"Po's a good fighter," Peach added. "And funny."

A side eye directed his way assessed him for comical attribute. He tried a smile. Hoped it didn't send her screaming.

Herbert cleared his throat. "I want to know more about this bear thing. Can you still skinwalk into your kangaroo?"

The next hour was spent talking about everything that had happened to him, with Maze finally getting the full version. Bored by the grownup talk, Peach fell asleep in his lap, a warm bundle of fur since she chose to be a cub to nap.

More than once he caught Maze staring at him, her brow knitted into a frown as if puzzled. He was feeling off kilter himself and not because of his panda.

There was something very real and comfortable about having a child put her trust in him enough to watch her while she slept. Something captivating about the way her mind worked. And when she looked at him... He wanted to give Peach anything she wanted.

And that went double for her mother.

There were only two caves set up for sleeping, and he got one of them to himself. A solid stretch of uninterrupted slumber saw him waking feeling energized and clear minded.

Time for him to make smarter decisions. Starting with not involving innocents in his problems.

He tiptoed out of his cave. The other one still had its leather curtain closed.

Before going to bed, he'd scouted two tunnels leading away from the lake. The one wide and welcoming, with scents galore. He chose the smallish one that he needed to heave himself through specifically because it had no smell at all. A hidden passage.

He'd grabbed his bug-out bag on his way out of the camp, moving quietly lest he wake them and have to make them understand this was for the best.

The tunnel twisted and churned before spitting him out amongst a rocky outcropping surrounded by stunted foliage—and Maze.

She sat on the ground with her back against a fat-boled tree, reading a book of all things.

"Took you long enough," she stated, placing her bookmark in her spot before stashing it in her pack.

"You were supposed to be sleeping."

"I did. And when I woke up, it occurred to me you might do something stupid and macho." She rolled her shoulders.

"And here I was going for stoic and brave. I'm going alone. It's for your own protection."

"I don't need you protecting me. I've been doing fine on my own."

"If not yourself, then Peach. You saw what happened. Being around me puts her in danger."

"What your mother is doing puts us all in danger." A somber reminder.

"You're stubborn."

"And you're still dumb. But cute." She popped to her feet and patted his cheek. "Now, if you're done whining, we've got miles to hike before we make it to the dune buggy I've got stashed."

"Did you say dune buggy?" If ever there was a moment to fall in love with a woman, this was it. The point of no return.

He loved her even more once she took the wheel and peeled through the barrens and the forests, jostling and bouncing them as she drove too fast, but not recklessly. She handled the buggy like a pro.

"When did you learn to drive like this?" Because, when he'd known her, she'd owned a battered Beetle and tended to drive at a sedate pace.

"A few years ago. I took defensive driving, followed by high-speed chase."

"Why?"

She cast him a quick glance. "Because."

"Because isn't an answer."

"I know."

In that moment she reminded him of his own reply when he'd announced he'd accepted a mercenary position and would be out of country for a while.

"Why do you have to go?"

"Because."

He now understood what a shitty reply that was.

Which was why the words tumbled out of him. "I didn't leave because I wanted to," he shouted over the growling engine.

"Even if you didn't want to, you decided. You. Not us, even though we were a couple." Her fingers tightened on the wheel.

"I had no choice. None of us did. Me and my brothers agreed to a two-year contract of missions to keep Uncle Kevyn alive instead of six feet under."

"What are you talking about?"

"Uncle K got caught with his paw in the cookie jar. The Council gave us a choice. Either we complete some missions equivalent to what Uncle K took or they would make an example of him."

"Let's say that's true. Why the heck wouldn't you have told me?"

"Because the deal was secret."

"I would have never told." She sounded offended, and with good reason.

"I know. But at the time, I was young and stupid. I thought everything would turn out fine. We'd do a few missions, you'd forgive me, and—"

"We'd live happily ever after? I save lives, Jakob. I don't take them. Did it even occur to you how I'd feel about dating a killer?"

He winced. "Not all of our jobs involved people getting whacked." And most of those who did get taken out deserved it.

"Even one is too many. And now is not the time to rehash the past."

Except there was no better time, because who knew what tomorrow would bring?

They reached a town where she accessed a garage, kept locked with keypad, where she traded the dune buggy for a two-door Honda Civic.

As she locked the garage, he couldn't help but say, "How many hidey spots do you have things stashed in?"

"A few," was her vague reply.

He was beginning to wonder why.

For this leg, she let him drive, and she pulled a new phone out of the glovebox. She had to plug it in, but as soon as she had signal, she was dialing.

He heard the reply. "Hamster House of Horror, Betty speaking."

"Hey, Betty. It's Maisy. I need a favor."

"Oh?"

Maisy sighed. "Sometimes the wheel spins so fast my hamster gets dizzy."

Which must have been code because Betty said, "What do you need?"

"Two tickets to Canada and transportation to FUCN'A. I'll need a suitcase, too, men's clothing, shirt size extra-large. Thirty-four inseam, thirty-six waist. Make that thirty-eight waist." She eyed him and made him conscious of the pounds he'd packed on.

He chewed on the bamboo utensils they'd found in a kitchen equipment store.

"Can you warn the Academy we've got an incoming

potential target? Confirmed tampering of genetics. The subject will require confidential one-on-one treatment and training."

"Oooh, sounds positively delicious. Is he cute?"

Maze ignored Betty's question. "I'll want full lab access and notify Dr. Nolan Master, as he is familiar with Mastermind's work."

"Did you find one of the escapees?"

"No. This is the work of the copycat."

"Don't you mean copy quokka?" he muttered.

After her call to Betty, he put in a quick one to his brothers. His da answered. "Who is this?"

"It's me, Dad."

"Boy, where are you? What happened to Maisy and the kid?"

"They're fine. We all are. We had a spot of trouble and hid in the bush until we could shake it."

"We were worried when we got word her place was torched," his father said softly. Not softly enough. Maisy stiffened.

"Ah shit. Did she lose everything?"

"Yeah. But you tell her we'll help her rebuild. Klaus already has some plans drawn up to give her something bigger, with a proper room for her to treat patients."

"I'm sure she'd like that."

A few more platitudes and he hung up. Maisy had her arms crossed.

"I'm sorry about your house."

"I know you are. And it's not your fault. I was planning to leave anyhow."

On her terms, with her things. This had to hurt. "We will rebuild."

"So I heard. Do you know how many times they've

offered already?" She snorted. "Guess I won't have a choice now. If I stick around."

"Where else would you go?" he asked, switching his gaze between her and the open road.

"The Academy offered me a position. Not only would it pay enough to allow me to live comfortably, I'd be doing what I love in a properly equipped environment. Peach could go to school with other kids like her and have the added benefit of learning at the Academy."

"But it's Canada." One thing to visit, but to live?

She rolled her shoulders. "Why not? I hear it's quite lovely."

"And cold."

"I have fur to keep me warm."

Technically, so did he. And a layer of pudge now, too. Poke it and die.

"What about your dad?"

She sighed. "He's the reason I haven't accepted yet. How can I tell him that not only is his daughter leaving but so is his best friend and granddaughter?"

"Maybe he would join you."

"As if he'd ever leave his home." She snorted.

"You never know." People would do a lot for love. Once upon a time, he'd given up the woman he cared for most in the world for family.

Now he was ready to forsake it all and even consider Canada if it meant a second chance with Maze.

Pity Mother didn't make him into a polar bear.

9

JAKOB KEPT TOSSING out mixed signals. One moment he was flirty and acting as if he'd seduce her, the next barely looking at her. Hot and cold. What did it mean? What did she want?

I want him.

She'd been with him less than two days, and yet that was all it had taken for all the old feelings to come rushing back, probably because they'd never left.

She loved Jakob Jones. Even if he was a dumbass. Even if he was a clumsy panda bear.

Being near him only reminded her of how good she felt with him. Which was why it had hurt so much when he'd let her down. He'd apologized. Said things would be different. That he was different.

Could she trust him? She wasn't sure if she wanted to risk finding out. Yet, here she was, making plans with him.

It took some string pulling, but within a day, they were on the long flight to Canada. At least they were in first class. They almost had the section to themselves, only three other passengers having paid for the upgrade. Just before the doors closed, about a half-dozen humans boarded and took seats in the row ahead of them and two of the rows across—at least she hoped they were human. With her shit sense of smell, who knew? Jakob certainly didn't act worried and relaxed in the last row of seats for their class, the partition wall just behind them.

As the plane taxied, Jakob said, "Tell me more about this Academy we're going to and why you're thinking of joining it. I thought you loved your practice."

"I do. Did. But I've got Peach to think about. She needs to go to school. To make friends. To be able to ride her bike to a store and buy herself some overpriced treats. To go to the movies and hang out at malls."

"You do know malls are pretty much a thing of the past."

Her nose wrinkled. "Don't remind me I'm getting old."

That brought his rich laughter. "Baby, we aren't even halfway to old. Still got plenty of life kicking around inside me." His smile was genuine and wide enough to pop that dimple she loved. The one she used to trace with her fingers.

"You're right; I am still young, and I should be doing more with my life."

"I'd say you've done plenty of good already. Everyone knows Doctor Williams."

She almost blushed, and she did her best not to squirm. "I'm not doing anything special."

"Other than helping anyone who shows up on your doorstep, including shitty ex-boyfriends."

"You weren't always entirely awful."

His grin turned rueful. "Good to know. So you want to give your kid a chance to explore somewhere a little more lively. Why not just move closer to a town instead of an entirely different continent?"

"I'd prefer to stay in Australia, but there are no labs that can help me do the kind of medical research I'm interested in." There were only human science centers, which, for obvious reasons, she couldn't exactly use. The only option would be to work for Jakob's mum, and she wasn't sure she could do the whole supervillain thing.

"It's so far."

"You're one to talk. Didn't your job take you around the world?"

"Yeah." He grimaced. "Which is how I know it's true when Dorothy said there's no place like home."

"I don't have a home anymore." A somber reminder that her home had been torched.

"And I am so sorry about that."

His contrite expression had her adding, "I don't blame you. Much."

"You should. I'm the reason your place is gone."

It was, along with all her things and memories. Thank goodness her dad had a stash of her most precious mementos, not to mention she'd created hidey holes in case something like this happened. It had been Peach's sad, "I don't want to say goodbye," while rubbing the wall a year ago that got her moving.

She wouldn't call her daughter psychic, but when Peach spoke about things that hadn't yet happened, she'd learned to listen. Peach had yet to be wrong.

So was she happy her home and practice got burned down? No, but she'd been expecting it. "Don't worry about it. This gives me the nudge I've been needing."

"More like a shove. I promise, once I'm done at the Academy, I will do whatever I can to help you and Peach settle somewhere, even if I have to build you a house myself."

She snorted. "You with a hammer? I'd better make sure I have some tincture for bruises."

"Are you implying I suck at home repair?"

"I'm sorry, do I need to be more obvious? You do suck at home repair. Or have you forgotten the spice rack?"

The reminder was of the hideous thing he'd built her for all her jars. He'd slaved over it, sanded it—too much in some places, giving it an uneven appearance—and then hung it without the benefit of a level so it sat at a tilt. When they broke up, she'd replaced it with a store-bought one that she installed herself—straight, she might add.

"I was still learning," he protested.

"Your skills lie in other directions," was her reply.

"I swear I've gotten better."

"Good for you."

"I really screwed shit up bad, didn't I?"

"Yes." They also weren't the same young people still learning their way in the world.

"Any chance you'll ever forgive me?"

"No." She said it quickly, lest her rapidly beating heart give her away.

"But…"

"You asked. And I said no." Never mind that she wanted to scream yes. She wasn't about to let him hurt her again. She'd maul him first. "Get some sleep." She turned away from him and closed her eyes.

The hum of the engines muffled conversation in the cabin. Soon the lights dimmed as well, but the gloom didn't lessen how ultra-conscious she remained of the man beside her.

A sucky nose didn't make her unaware of his scent. He

filled her senses. Familiar and yet different. The proximity of him enough to arouse.

She eyed the blanket he'd lain over her when the flight attendant handed them out. Loose enough to hide anything.

She closed her eyes. What was she thinking? She was thinking she wouldn't mind sticking her hand on his thigh and seeing what happened.

He might have sucked at handiwork, but his fingers never failed to please. She squirmed and pressed her thighs together. Looked out her window but saw nothing. They were flying at night, meaning the dim lighting cast her reflection on the glass against the darkness outside. She could see one of the humans in the next row glancing her way then pretending to watch their mini television again.

She shifted, trying to get comfortable. They were less than two hours into a twenty-one-hour flight. She really should sleep.

Jakob sighed.

Loudly.

"You awake?" he whisper-shouted.

She kept her eyes closed and her breathing even.

"Maze?"

She groaned and rolled her head over to glare at him. "What?"

"I can't sleep."

"Of course, you can. You're part panda now. They sleep like twenty-three hours a day."

"I know, I should be napping, and I'm tired, but…" The reply trailed off.

"But what? Close your eyes and try."

"I don't like closing them."

"Why?" she asked softly. "What happens when you close your eyes?"

It took a moment for her to hear his faint reply. "I panic that I'll wake up months later again with no idea of what happened. Feeling the same and different at once. Waking up as someone else."

"You're still Jakob Jones."

"Am I?"

He glanced down at the hands he was wringing in his lap. His vulnerability poked at her.

"If you're not Jakob, then you are a kick-ass imitation. You look the same. Sound the same."

"I don't smell the same, though," he reminded.

"And?"

"And I'm a bear," he grumbled in a low tone.

"A cute one according to Peach."

"Not helping."

"Aren't I? Let me ask, am I treating you differently than you expected?"

"Actually, you are being nicer than I could have hoped for. A part of me was convinced you'd slam the door in my face or use your magic to give me the permanent runs."

"I still might."

He snorted. "You would never intentionally hurt anyone."

"Don't be so sure of that." She'd had a few incidences that made her revise her stance on doing harm. She realized she wasn't willing to be hurt or see those she loved hurt either.

"Someone tried to hurt you." He growled softly, his agitation clear as he showed a perception that read between the words.

"An addict. And a cryptid, too. When I wouldn't give him narcotics, he attacked me."

Jakob trembled. "Tell me you killed him."

"No. I put him to sleep and drove him to town. Left him by a hostel."

"And he came back."

"He did," she murmured. "It was a few days after I got Peach."

Her little girl had tried to warn her, pointing a finger at the door and saying, "Bah. Bah." Turned out she meant bad. But Maisy hadn't known, and that addict had come in, eyes wild, brandishing a knife.

He'd threatened little fuzz.

A mama bear had nothing on a panther mom who lost her shit.

After that incident, she learned to protect herself. And when Peach spoke, she listened.

"I'm sorry you had to deal with that yourself."

"Why apologize? It had nothing to do with you."

"Didn't it, though? If I'd stayed, I'd have been there to handle it, and you would have never had to deal with that ugly side of the world."

She snorted. "The patriarchy is alive and well."

"How about chivalry isn't dead?" was his hot retort. "Or is it really that shameful that I'd want to protect someone I care about?" He spoke in the present tense as if he still did.

"But you didn't protect me. *I* did. And I will continue to defend myself and Peach."

"I didn't mean to say you couldn't."

She sighed. "I know." Yet she wanted to pick a fight. It was the only way to resist his allure. "You need to rest."

"I want to. I just can't seem to manage it."

"Is there anything that would help?"

"Cuddle me."

"Excuse me?"

"Snuggle me. Hold me. I used to have the best sleep wrapped around you."

The reminder of their naked limbs entwined had her hotly exclaiming, "Is this a ploy for sex?"

"Sex would make me feel better."

"Jakob!" she squeaked.

"What? Just saying it would," he protested.

"Not the time or place," she said pertly, hoping he didn't see her blush because she'd been thinking about the same thing a moment ago.

"We never did join the mile-high club."

"And we aren't going to start today. Go to sleep."

He closed his eyes and held himself rigid.

She'd never thought to see him scared. She reached over and grabbed his hand. "I'm here." Maybe not the reassurance he wanted, but apparently enough to put him to sleep.

She, on the other hand, remained awake. And when the cabin grew quiet, she slipped past Jakob to use the washroom. When she exited the tiny cubicle, she noticed the stewardess preparing her trolley with water, coffee, tea, and snacks.

A single pair of eyes from the human sitting in the row in front of hers flicked to her quickly, almost furtively, then back down again. Everyone else seemed to be studiously pretending she wasn't there.

It tickled her paranoia.

She leaned into the galley. "Excuse me, ma'am?"

"Yes?" The older stewardess had her gray-streaked blonde hair pulled back, the severe style at odds with the smile.

"I don't suppose you have an apple?"

"Of course. Give me a moment."

Maisy braced herself on the cart while the woman turned her back. It took a moment of rummaging before Maisy was handed the apple and returned to her seat.

As the stewardess rolled down the aisle with her offerings, Jakob roused and perked up at the sight of food.

Maisy leaned close. "You don't want anything."

"But I'm hungry and thirsty."

"Trust me. You don't want anything on that cart." She bent down and pulled free two water bottles and some bamboo shoots from her knapsack.

His eyes widened in delight. He leaned back and tried to be discreet about the fact he was chewing on bamboo, observing the stewardess as she served everyone, waving her on when she reached them.

Within half an hour, there was a lineup to the bathroom and a smell even her pathetic nose couldn't miss.

Jakob had the bottom half of his face tucked into his shirt. "I've heard of bad airline food, but this is crazy."

"It was necessary."

"What did you do?" he muttered.

"I'm pretty sure those last-minute passengers are human-smelling cryptids. I needed them preoccupied."

"So you gave them all the shits?"

"I'm sorry, was I supposed to kill them on a plane full of witnesses?"

"What makes you think they're bad guys?" Jakob adopted Peach's terminology. Or was it just that mentally he was closer to Peach's age than her own?

"Call it a hunch." Or the fact that they smelled too

human, and too alike. As if they all wore the same human essence cologne.

No one was watching them by the time the plane landed, and those that were sick were immediately placed in quarantine. Maisy managed to avoid it by claiming they'd not partaken of any food or snacks provided on board and flashing her medical credentials.

They made it through customs quicker than expected and soon were on the outside curb, looking for their ride.

"Over there." Jakob pointed to a sign labelled "Jones."

As she headed for the man wearing a chauffeur's cap, she took note of other people on the sidewalk. A family holding tight to some wailing children. Business types in suits, faces glued to their phones, somehow managing to walk and tap at the same time. A grizzly-faced fellow with a distinct furry vibe, wearing a plaid shirt, sauntering slowly along.

She turned back as the man with the sign said, "Are you Jakob Jones?"

"Yup."

"If you'll follow me." The driver, who smelled very strongly of a cologne that stifled the senses, didn't offer to grab their bags as he led them from the busy pick-up area to the parking garage.

They went to the top deck, where only a few vehicles sat parked. There was not another living soul in sight. The driver aimed for a sedan with tinted windows. He held out the key fob, the lights flashed and the trunk popped open.

"Put your stuff in the back," their chauffeur ordered.

Maisy, while not a weak damsel, was surprised at the lack of an offer to help. From the corner of her eye, she saw a door opening on one of the other cars.

Jakob swung his duffel into the trunk, but when he went to grab Maisy's, his eyes widened. "Behind—"

She ducked before he finished his warning, avoiding the needle coming her way. But that was only half of the problem. Jakob dove at their chauffeur, who'd pulled another needle, and they hit the ground, wrestling.

Dashing past the newcomer with his jabbing weapon, she scrounged in her pockets, not having been able to bring much on board, not with the new flight safety rules. The only reason she had a diuretic to rub on that serving trolley was because she always kept a dose of it inside her medallion.

At this point in time, though, she had nothing but her wits. She flipped to walk backwards as the newcomer pulled a gun and stalked her. "Come with us quietly and no one gets hurt."

One of the first things Maisy had taught Peach when she went on her self-defense kick was to never go with anyone without fighting. Best to be as loud and feisty as possible.

With that in mind, she ran for the thug, baring teeth and popping some claws. He might have a gun, but she was counting on the fact he wouldn't use it.

As expected, the gun lifted, and he braced for impact as she barreled for him. At the last moment, he stepped to the side, and she stumbled past, tripping over the foot he extended. She hit the ground on the heels of her palms and growled. She'd let panic overcome her lessons. She rolled in time to avoid the descending needle. Before he could recover from his jab, she swiped claws across his thigh.

He yelled and dropped his needle to put his hand on the wound, but he also fired his gun.

Pop!

The tranquilizing bullet hit the ground and shattered, but the syringe remained intact. She scrabbled for it and wrapped her fingers around it and then swung it like a weapon.

She didn't miss, and yet the needle bent as it hit hardened skin.

The thug, with his shifting features, smiled with layers of crocodile teeth. "That tickled."

"Does this?" She kicked him in the balls, and he gasped, bending over double. She chopped at his head and brought up her knee at the same time. Winced at the crunch of cartilage and hoped he wouldn't bleed too badly over her clothes.

"Bitch!"

"Compare me to a dog will you." She didn't feel bad as she raked her claws over his shoulder, not quite shredding flesh, but instinct had him pulling away.

Before she could lunge in and incapacitate him, someone grabbed her in a bear hug that crushed her ribs and made it hard to breathe.

Crocodile man stood, his face a bleeding mess, and smiled again. Whatever that smirk meant, he never got to accomplish it because he suddenly hit the ground and jiggled. She noticed a wire stringing from him to the man in plaid from downstairs, who held a taser.

"Let her go," the new stranger said slowly.

"Don't come near or she gets it," threatened her hugging thug, giving her ribcage a squeeze.

"You heard the guy. Let Maze go!" Jakob snarled a second before the grip on her slackened.

She turned to see Jakob holding her assailant in a head lock. Which was perfect for the man in plaid, who took his time sauntering over to shove one of the needles into the thug. In seconds, Hug-a-thug slumped. Their fake chauffeur groaned on the ground, so they jabbed him too.

"We shouldn't leave these here," the man in plaid said.

Understanding what he needed, they jumped to help. Within a minute, all three bodies were stowed in the boot of the car.

The grizzly guy slammed the sedan's trunk shut and smiled. "Welcome to Canada, eh."

❧ 10 ❧

AFTER THAT EXCITEMENT, they didn't argue when their real chauffeur, the plaid-wearing Tom, suggested they grab some Timmies. For the non-Canadian, that meant grabbing a coffee and a maple-flavored donut from a drive-thru that had a stream of cars when they entered and a stream once they left.

During this time, Tom made slow conversation. Very slow, which was normal given his sloth nature.

"How was the flight?"

"Explosive?" Jakob joked from his spot in the front seat. Maisy sat in the back, checking mail and messages from her father and daughter.

"Someone is after you," Tom observed.

"And obviously knew we were coming here. The Academy might not be safe."

Tom uttered a noise. "Nowhere safer."

"And they're aware we're coming in hot," Maisy advised from the back seat. "Don't worry about the Academy. It is one of the most protected places in the world."

"Got the best of the best working there," Tom added.

"Are you a FUC agent?" Jakob asked the man.

"Not quite. Used to be a gumshoe with my pal, Everett. Did some odd jobs for FUC every so often. But once my pal met Dawn, and after that fiasco with Joey, we thought it was time for a change in career. Something that would afford more nap time." Tom's half-shut eyes made Jakob wonder if the man was currently missing his.

Maze leaned forward. "I've read about Dawn. Dr. Manners sent her file to ask my opinion on her condition, and I met her on my last visit."

That drew Jakob's attention. "Is something wrong with this Dawn person?"

"Mastermind." A one-word answer from Tom that explained a lot.

But Maisy added to it. "The serum causes behavioral and physical changes. In Dawn's case, a violent bloodlust that she can't always control. Given she's a gentle minded, doe, the change has caused issues."

"Were you able to help her?"

Maze shook her head. "What Mastermind managed to do to Dawn happened at a cellular level. Walking it back would involve much uncertainty and danger."

"Meaning I'm screwed," he said in a low tone.

"Depends on your point of view," was Tom's sage offering. "Dawn might have some issues to deal with, but she's still found happiness."

It took Tom so long to say this that Jakob had a chance to wonder what the worst thing was that could happen if he remained a bear.

Mockery by his family. But that happened no matter what anyhow.

A loss of ability because of the different body, but at the same time, he'd gain new skills.

He tried to think of some more bad points. He was kind of coming up dry.

As they went from the airport to the Academy, Tom predictably drove under the speed limit and made no attempt to beat the GPS-projected trip time. Never played that game? It was simple. Enter a destination, make note of the trip finder's arrival time, and then drive—sometimes a bit above the speed limit—and see by how many minutes you could beat it.

Currently his Uncle Klaus held the record. A three-hour trip in under one. Da claimed the fact Klaus avoided the bridge and went across the river using a barge negated the record-setting time shave. But really Da was just mad because it knocked him out of first place.

Tom slowed even more so they almost crawled as they reached an electronic gate with possibly more security than the White House. Not all of the surveillance was visible. There were the expected cameras bolted at the top of the gate on either side, alternating their rotation, while a third sat in the middle and didn't move at all.

A row of spikes lay flat across the opening, ready to spring and impale any unauthorized vehicles.

There was a guardhouse set off to the side, manned by a fellow with bulging eyes and a prominent Adam's apple. Dressed in emerald green trimmed in black, he sat in the booth, appearing benign and unarmed, yet Jakob would wager he wasn't defenseless. A place like the Academy with shifters of all castes learning to be the best animal they could be needed stiff protection. Especially now, given his mom had spilled the beans and told the world about their existence.

The only lucky thing was no one took her seriously. The media found all kinds of experts to debunk everything she'd said and what was seen. He'd wager the Council had helped with that. It behooved them to put the shifter back in its hidden cage. Imagine a world where they tried to coexist with humans.

He knew their history. It never ended well for anyone. Jakob could only hope the furor died down and things went back to normal. However, he highly doubted his mother would give up so easily. Not to mention there was a possibility the media provided cover while the government dug deeper into the shifter secret.

If they were on to the existence of cryptids... What would the governments do with that information?

Culling came to mind. Others believed they'd be forced to register. Maybe even pay extra taxes to counter their environmental footprint. Because if they got classified as animals, then it wasn't farfetched to imagine that there could be a fee imposed on their poop. After all, they'd done it to the farmers who actually fed the humans.

Why did his mother have to threaten their existence? Why couldn't the woman have a normal midlife crisis like everyone else?

The car passed through the gate, and Tom crawled up the long drive, giving them a restricted view, given the thick shrubbery that lined the two-sided driveway. Not much to see, so why did he feel nervous? The flip-flops in his stomach were usually reserved for when he was about to be do something heroic—and stupid.

This wasn't dangerous or life threatening. His mouth still dried as the drive curved into a massive roundabout around a huge stone fountain. People played in the spraying water that emerged from the top of a spire.

Tom pulled to a stop by the curb and turned slowly.

"We're here, folks." The smile took forever to stretch his lips.

It reminded Jakob of what Uncle Kevyn said of the sloth. *"They are the most loyal and steady of the furry cryptids. If you don't mind aging while you wait for them to do something."*

"Thanks." Jakob eyed the massive building and did his best to ignore his clenched fists. Nothing to fear. The structure looked like a regular school, make that a college or university with its girth that sprawled into wings. Old stone for the front, more uniform concrete polished blocks for the branches. A mixture of old and new architecture.

Off to the sides of the building were green fields, scattered copses of trees, more buildings. ARSHOL sprawled over a ridiculous number of hectares, although on paper apparently there were seven properties with different owners. Shifters were always cautious to not draw attention.

Always hiding. Would that ever end?

"This place is huge," he said as Maisy joined him to stand at the steps to the school.

"And that's just the tip of the installation. You should see the subterranean component."

The fact there was more underground boggled the mind.

Tom joined them. "Impressive, eh."

"Very."

The fact shifters had their own training school was amazing. Used to be FUC and the other agencies sent their cryptid agents to the human schools that taught law enforcement and combat skills. Some even joined the military to get the education they needed, and once they'd milked all the knowledge, it eased them into FUC.

"And this is only one of three. We've got one started now in the Swiss Alps and another in South America."

"We could use one down under," Jakob noted.

"I'm sure the Council would be amenable if they could find the right people to run it." Tom eyed him, and Jakob shook his head.

"Oh no, don't look at me. I am not anything close to a dean."

"What about teacher? The academies need plenty of those."

The very idea had Jakob snorting. "And teach what? I barely passed high school."

"You have other skills," Tom noted.

"Such as? The only thing I know how to do is fight, but that was before I turned into something else."

"There's other things you could teach, like the proper way to rappel out of a helicopter."

"I only learned that because my brother shoved me off a helicopter in the middle of a firefight."

"And can therefore speak from experience. We'd like to offer more courses on strategy. How to plan a successful extraction. What you should bring on a mission."

"What you're suggesting is crazy. Me a teacher?" The idea intrigued more than it should have.

"It's got its perks," Tom drawled.

"But it would require him staying in one place," was Maze's pert reply.

Jakob glanced at her. "I'm not averse to settling down." Not anymore.

A big man emerged from the building. His suit had to be tailor made given it fit the massive chest with ease. He had his hair trimmed short and his jaw clean shaven.

Jakob recognized the man as Chase Brownsmith. "I didn't know Chase was here."

"Course he is. He basically runs the place," Tom declared.

"Since when?" Used to be Chase worked for FUC as a lawyer and support to his wife, one of their top-ranked agents.

"He started out part time but recently moved here to work full time, at least until we can find a proper replacement. In the meantime, he and his family live in the dean's home." Tom pointed east. "We've got a whole new development going in to ensure adequate housing for the Academy staff."

"Sounds like you've thought of everything."

"Yup."

As Chase neared, Jakob caught a hint of something sweet and sticky. He fingered the stick of bamboo in his pocket, as he suddenly got an urge to find a pot of honey gold and dip the sliver in it. Probably delicious.

Chase came to a halt in front of them and gave them a nod. "Jakob, nice to see you again."

"Hey, Chase. Where's your wife and the little joey?"

He referred to the child Chase and Miranda had together. He'd met the pair when they ended up in Australia tracking one of Mastermind's subjects, who ended up marrying one of his brothers. Mari was expecting their chick to hatch any day now.

"Miranda will be along shortly. Woman can't sit still for a second these days." Chase shook his head. He eyed Maisy. "You must be Dr. Williams. I've heard excellent things about your work."

"You have?" Jakob queried. He'd always known Maze

was good at her job but never realized she did more than just the hands-on.

"Dr. Williams has been providing us with some excellent research notes on her study of family recipes passed down in Australia. Her insight really helped our labs in several cases. It's a pleasure to finally meet you." His big hand engulfed hers.

"Thank you." Maisy couldn't hide her blush.

"I don't suppose you're here to accept our offer?" Chase asked hopefully. "We'd love for you to come work for the Academy."

"I'm still thinking about it. Actually, the real reason I'm here is because of Jakob."

"The report I received was vague about his problem." Chase eyed Jakob. "But now that he's here, I think I'm grasping his dilemma. Your scent... It's not the same as I recall. If I didn't know better, I'd say—"

"I smell human. I know." Jakob's lips turned down.

"You can't shift anymore?" Tom blurted out, joining the conversation and more rapidly than anything else he'd done thus far.

"I can shift, just not into a kangaroo."

"Then what do you turn into?" Chase asked.

"A bear," he huffed.

That wrinkled Chase's nose. "You don't have the scent of a bear."

"Which is only part of the weirdness," Maisy declared. "But I can assure you, despite what your nose might be saying, Jakob most definitely turns into an enormous panda."

"You've seen it?" Chase sounded skeptical.

She nodded. "I was there when it happened, and I will

add the man goes through bamboo like a gambling addict through lottery tickets."

The very reminder by Maisy had him pulling forth a chunk and sticking it between his lips for a nice crunch.

"If you're here hoping our labs can change you back, then I will have to disappoint. We've yet to reverse any effects."

"I'm aware," Jakob said, a touch sourly. "And that's not why I came. I suck in my new body. I can't fight. I can barely walk without falling. I need help figuring out how to not die because I'm so damned clumsy."

Chase laughed. "In other words, you want lessons on being a bear. I think we can manage that. Currently, I'm the only bear on campus, but between me and a few others, like Viktor, who is king when it comes to shooting, we should be able to teach you a thing or two."

"I'd appreciate it." If he was stuck being a panda, then he wanted to be a kick-ass version. Not the comic relief who died first.

"Take today to get settled in. We'll start tomorrow. First, how about a mini tour of the campus so you know what's going on? The building at my back"—Chase swept his hand—"is the Academy's main headquarters."

"Call it like the kids do, honey bear. Welcome to WANC, short for Working and Administration Networking Core." Miranda popped into view, having arrived downwind from them.

She jogged in place, jiggling a big round belly that projected enough that Jakob wondered how she remained upright. By Miranda's side was her mini me, Baby Kelly, who was more toddler than baby now. With her blonde hair in pigtails, the child was the spitting image of her mother.

"Miranda." Jakob greeted her. "It's nice to see you again. When is the baby due?" And shouldn't the woman try standing still? What if she jostled the baby out early?

"Junior will be coming anytime now." Miranda kept bouncing. "I can't wait. I'm not used to slowing down."

A bunny's idea of a slow pace was like supersonic to the sloth, who was removing their luggage from the trunk. "Where am I taking them?" asked Tom, lifting the bags.

"The guesthouse since they're only here for a short time," Miranda stated, doing some jumping jacks. "I'll take them over. Kelly, you go with Daddy and get some lunch."

"Do I haf to?" The lower lip jutted.

"Growing girls need their vitamin C. Let's go. Hop. Hop."

"Fro me!" the little girl cried, bouncing and clapping her hands.

"Get ready to catch, honey." Miranda crouched and held out her cupped fingers.

The little girl stepped into the linked palms and was vaulted into the air. Kelly flew, squealing with delight. Chase held up an arm and snared his kid.

Not that Jakob knew that would happen. The moment the kid went airborne, he dove to the ground, ready to act as a cushion.

Chase eyed him and grunted. "Single, eh?"

"For the moment," Jakob replied, rolling to his feet. He'd lost that springiness he used to have. His movements were slower, more ponderous, more bearlike.

Kelly canted her head and eyed Maisy. "You smell like a kitty."

"And you smell like a baby bunny. Delicious. Reminds

me of the wild hares I hunted with my dad, spitted over an open fire."

"Maisy!" Jakob was the one to sound shocked.

Whereas Kelly giggled and clapped her hands. "Chomp. Chomp."

Maisy cast him a wink. "She knows I'm joking."

Jakob hoped so because he'd heard stories about Miranda, the saber-toothed bunny. They had to be exaggerated. Look at the woman. She didn't even reach Maisy's chin. "Let's not discuss the eating of people's children, especially in front of them."

"But they're delicious when baked in some honey," Miranda said, completely deadpan. "I love crunching me some toes."

Kelly squealed as Miranda dove for her feet and opened her mouth as if to bite them. The tyke clambered up her father to sit, giggling, astride his shoulders.

Seeing Maisy's soft expression made Jakob think of Peach. She was just as cute, but he would never pretend to eat her. He never wanted her to be scared. Not of him or anyone.

"If we're done discussing the eating of my sweet baby girl, perhaps we could get on with the tour so I can get back to my paperwork," Chase said in a low rumble.

"You and your papers," Miranda moaned.

"Quiet about my work, woman. Be a good wife and bake me a pie."

It was said quite seriously, and for a moment, Jakob wondered if Miranda would bite off Chase's head for the sexist demand.

Instead, her laughter proved bright and shining. "You are such a bad bear, Chase Brownsmith. But you'll get your pie. Later." The wink was not the least bit subtle. She turned to Maisy and Jakob. "If you'll follow me, I will give you the quick tour."

"I highly doubt they want to keep pace with you. How about you take the cart?"

"I'd rather run. Anyone care to join me?" She bounced on the balls of her feet.

"Me! Me!" Kelly bounced.

"You're supposed to go with Daddy."

The pouty lip and big eyes squashed that idea. "Pretty pw-ease, Mummy?"

"Only if you stay close to Uncle Tom. We don't need you teasing the lions again."

"Yay."

Despite the offer, only Miranda chose to go on foot, easily keeping pace with the golf cart driven by Tom, who ended up with Kelly in his lap. Jakob sat beside him, making the poor cart groan, while Maisy perched on the back, squished beside their luggage, her legs dangling.

Miranda provided a running commentary as they followed the paved path. "Training fields. The public ones. We also have hidden arenas so that people can practice in their other forms."

They went past habitats ranging from a massive greenhouse structure housing the tropics to a marsh and a forest. Even a desert-like space that also served as sand traps on a golf course.

At the end of the tour, Jakob was even more impressed than before. This went beyond any school he'd ever imagined. The equipment available, the possibilities... Jakob and his brothers had trained with humans and had to learn on their own how to incorporate their other selves to the best advantage. The Academy melded both components, swapping lessons between the shapes, fine-tuning its students into soldiers.

"You're preparing for a war," Jakob muttered as they passed the training field with its mock war game and headed back for the main area.

Tom kept his eyes ahead as he said, "Ayuh, although we're hoping it won't happen. But times are a changing. Humans aren't as blind as they used to be."

"And then you have my mother telling them point-blank we exist."

"Even without her interference, it would have happened. The world is waking up and taking notice in ways we never imagined. It is only a matter of time before we might be forced to defend ourselves," Tom said, his tone quite somber.

Might not be long before they'd have to fight. Jakob might not want to start a war with humans, but he also wouldn't allow anyone to deny him his right to exist.

As they approached WANC, Miranda dropped back and kept pace with the golf cart. "I'm going to make myself a fresh-pressed carrot juice and have a piece of cake."

"Me too!" A tiny body sailed from the cart and hit the ground with her knees bent before bolting.

Tom drove just past the main building to a two-story house and pulled up in front. "Guest quarters."

He stepped out of his seat, and the cart almost tipped before Jakob had the sense to throw himself out the other side. He grabbed the suitcase Maisy had arranged to have for him and would have grabbed hers too, but Tom actually got it first. They entered the home, and it was as you'd expect with a large living room to one side, dining room on the other.

"Kitchen's at the back," Tom remarked. "Fridge and pantry have been stocked with food, but if it's missing something, send us a note. Someone will get it for you."

"He'll need bamboo," Maisy stated, saving Jakob the embarrassment of asking for his odd snack.

"Already done. We've got some tender shoots in the fridge, some crunchy stalks in the fruit bowl on the counter, and some salted version on the nightstand of his room. We've provided an array of smoked meats. The boar is especially tasty."

Separate rooms. He shouldn't have been surprised. They parted in the hallway on the second floor, and he entered his room and immediately went for the salted treats.

Munching on a stalk, he paced his room. Some of his nerves had calmed when he'd seen the campus. He'd come to the right place to learn. Now he just had to get over the shame of not being himself.

Given it had been more than a day since he'd talked to his family, he gave them a shout.

His Uncle Klaus answered. "Jones House of Pleasure."

"You know Da hates it when you do that."

"Then your da shouldn't have left me in charge."

"Where is he?"

"Better question is, where are you? The number you're calling from is based in Canada."

"Because I'm currently visiting."

"Why?" A blunt query. "You hate the cold."

"The weather's not bad, actually." In the teens Celsius, making it comfortable still.

"Why does your call show it originating from the FUC Academy?" No surprise Uncle ran a trace on what should have been a safe line.

"Because I'm visiting the campus for the next little while."

"Why?" Again, his uncle didn't bother beating around the bush.

But Jakob wasn't ready for the truth. "Thinking about a career change. Maybe becoming a teacher."

The laughter had him frowning at the phone as he held it away from his ear.

"I don't see why that's so funny."

"You. A teacher." Uncle Klaus snorted.

"Some people think I have skills that should be shared."

"You're a man of action. Not a pencil pusher behind a desk."

"How would you know?" Jakob wasn't sure anymore what he wanted. He did know his current life didn't fulfill him. He needed a change.

"A Jones is meant for action."

"Jax and Jeb seem pretty happy with their choices in life."

Jax had never been the mercenary sort. As for Jeb, he'd changed his life around when he met Nev.

"They caved to their women. Don't make the same mistake, boy. Don't let yourself be chained. Take it from me." From a man who was a confirmed bachelor, with no kids of his own.

"You saying Da regretted marrying Mum and having us?" The question put his uncle in a bind, but Jakob enjoyed the stammering.

"Course not. Er, you boys are a fine lot."

"You're a horrible liar. Anyhow, I called just to let you know I was okay. How is the mission to capture Mum going?"

"It's going. That woman is more slippery than a pig rubbed in grease."

He knew better than to ask why anyone would rub a pig in grease.

Knock. Knock.

"I gotta go. Tell Da and my brothers that I'm good."

"Will do."

He hung up and answered the next knock to see Chase. The bear had swapped the suit for trackpants and a T-shirt.

"You ready for your first lesson?" Chase asked.

"I thought we were starting tomorrow."

Chase eyed him. "You really want to wait that long?"

He shook his head.

"Then let's go."

Chase's idea of lessons involved making him shift, muttering, *"Holy shit, you're huge,"* and then turning into a grizzly. Which also gave him some size. Chase then spent the afternoon knocking his ass down on a mat over and over again. Enough times that it hurt. But by the time suppertime rolled around, Jakob had managed to pin Chase once.

Then they broke for dinner, a raucous affair in a massive cafeteria with dozens coming and going. Miranda actually sat for a second to eat an astonishing amount of food.

Looking around, Jakob took in the many faces, but one in particular was missing.

"Where's Maze?" he asked Tom, who sat across him.

"Downstairs in the lab." The man pointed.

"Oh." He shouldn't have been surprised she'd gone off to do her own thing.

Bummed, he grabbed some of the fresh bamboo they'd

provided on a side plate and discovered honey truly was delicious on bamboo and everything else it was drizzled on.

After dinner, he took a jar of honey and a bag of bamboo to his room and proceeded to eat it, wondering what he could do to win Maze over.

11

Maisy left her room minutes after dropping her bag, spending only a quick moment splashing her face to wipe away the travel fatigue. She pulled the samples she'd smuggled into the country from out of the makeup case she'd stored them in. Would they find any answers in the blood? With the help of the most up-to-date equipment and some of the sharpest minds, she hoped to soon find out.

The case with its vials was tucked into a satchel, and with only a slightly longing look at the bed and those comfy-looking pillows, she left. In the hall, she glanced at Jakob's door but didn't knock. What purpose would it serve? He was here for one thing. She had come for another.

It was best this way.

Needing to stretch her legs, she headed to the main building on foot, making note of the interesting sections in the Academy, like the alchemy lab and the kitchens. Something for everyone, including a golf course with some wicked sand traps. The handbook had a warning about not playing in them. Apparently, they had a sandworm who tunneled through the sand leaving weak spots that could swallow a person whole.

The man-made lake she passed was beautiful. According to what she'd learned, it provided its own ecosystem. The bottom was lined with buildings built ahead of time inside a massive pit before being flooded. It wasn't just the fish shifters that went to that part of the school. A few dolphin shifters, freshwater lobster shifters, and even a trio of selkies attended the aquatic classes.

Glancing overhead, she noticed there was a cloud that seemed to more or less hover over the campus. Shapes sometimes darted from the fluffy cumulus. A campus in the sky with lots of flying creatures?

Yummy.

Birds and dangly bits were weaknesses. Although, she'd learned her lesson when it came to running with loose string because it usually ended in tragedy for the unravelling sweater.

The main building, WANC, projected into the sky. It had nice girth, a solid presence pulsing with life. A constant flow of students ebbed in and out.

All the people she passed gave her a nod or a smile. Dude with the shades on was a raccoon, the girl in pigtails an actual pig, the lanky one with the longish, dirty-blond hair barely more than a colt.

Given Maisy's age in her thirties, they probably assumed she was staff. Once inside, she found herself trying to remember where to go. She'd only visited briefly once before. The Academy had reached out to her after the incident with a hybrid chameleon named Joey. She'd not been able to do much; however, the Academy had still called upon her a few times after for help and most recently had headhunted her.

They wanted her to work for them.

Surrounded for a second time by the vibrant energy on the campus, she would admit to being tempted. The vitality in the place was off the charts, but it was what hid below the earth that made her scientist heart beat faster.

The elevator had regular buttons for the top floors. She placed her hand on the spot above the keypad, the wood grain seamless from the rest. The doors closed, and the wall outlined the contour of her fingers in light.

"Floor number?" a soft voice queried.

"The labs, please."

The elevator didn't jolt as it slid down. The ride was smooth except for the weightless sensation in her stomach.

Whoosh. The doors slid open on an empty room with a closed door. She stepped in and waited. *Whir.* The elevator left, and grills opened in the walls. The same voice of the elevator said, "Strip and place your clothing and belongings in the bin."

A drawer slid out of the wall. She pulled out the case of samples and placed it atop the pile she put inside.

Whir, click. The drawer disappeared, and she stood naked and waiting.

Despite knowing what would happen, she still grimaced as a powdery substance emerged from the walls, followed by a brisk blowing, which began cold and then got hot. Almost too hot to handle. Decontamination level one.

Only once the wind died down, and her hair sported more wisps than she could quickly fix, did the door click and open. On to the next layer of protection. There were three decontamination protocols in total before she could enter the lab proper wearing her clothes, which had gone through their own detoxing. It might seem like overkill. After all cryptids were resistant to disease.

But the things they studied could be fragile. Accurate results required clean environments. The labs were partitioned with glass, the giant windows enclosing each section, sealing them hermetically against contamination or a dangerous leak.

This was where they studied potential biological hazards and tried to understand what Mastermind's potion had done. How had she changed her subjects? Could it be reversed? Could aspects of it be used for good?

They already knew its potential for evil. Mastermind had paved the way when it came to depravity with her experiments. But it didn't end when she died. Next came Kole, in cahoots with the ex-Mrs. Jones. What possessed them to devise a way to change humans and develop the scent thing, where they couldn't tell shifter from non-shifter anymore? Even she, with her weak sense of smell, never realized how much she still relied on it.

What else did the devious Mrs. Jones plan to do? Could she get any more depraved than changing her own son into something else? Poor Jakob. Maisy couldn't imagine not being her panther. What if she'd been the one caught and turned into something horrid like a chipmunk? From predator to prey... She didn't want to become anyone's squeaky toy.

"You must be Maisy Williams." A man with an impressive head of blond hair emerged from a lab with a bright white smile. "At last we meet in person. I'm Dr. Nolan Manners."

She took the hand he offered and shook it. "Thanks for letting me bring the samples." She waggled the box. A good thing she'd thought to grab blood and tissue from the four thugs who attacked. Pity she couldn't get any from the passengers on the plane.

"I have to admit to being intrigued. A shifter with no scent. It seems impossible."

"It's not natural," she agreed. "You'll get to experience it, though, if you take a moment to meet with Jakob."

"Ah yes, the Jones fellow who is now a panda instead of a kangaroo. Truly remarkable. Good job bringing him here for study. We'll give him today to settle in before we start tests." Nolan rubbed his hands, clearly enthusiastic about the idea.

Maisy balked. "I didn't bring Jakob here for you to poke him like a lab rat. I suggested the Academy because he needs help figuring out his panda side."

"And he'll receive all the aid he requires, but you can't deny he provides us with the perfect opportunity to study what his mother did."

The fact that Nolan made sense didn't alleviate her sudden guilt. She'd not thought about the fact he'd be a test subject. "I'm not sure he'll agree."

"If he's not keen, then perhaps we can convince him because the more we learn, the better equipped we'll be to deal with the victims of Mrs. Jones's experiments."

"Can we stop calling her Mrs. Jones?" That woman had stopped being a mother and wife the day she stepped out on her family to start a career as an evil mad doctor scientist.

"Technically, she never did divorce."

"She was declared dead. I'd say that's enough," Maisy pointed out.

"We can refer to her as per her casefile name, Mother Q."

"Do we know where she is?" she asked, following Nolan into one of the sterile rooms. She set the case down beside a centrifuge, a machine to separate the components in blood.

"Not currently. A tip FUC followed turned out to be gas."

"Jakob said his family was planning to raid her compound the last time they spoke."

"They did. It was a joint operation with FUC that unfortunately failed. She slipped away before we infiltrated."

"That woman is more slippery than an intestine," she grumbled.

"And has a lot to answer for. Hopefully she'll cooperate with the doctors when we find her. Some of the things she's managed to accomplish are incredible."

"That almost sounds admiring," she accused.

"The woman accomplished the impossible."

"I'll tell you what, Jakob doesn't think his mother's meddling is incredible."

That stifled Nolan's eager expression. "I didn't mean to make light of his situation. It is a horrifying thing to have one's intimate self replaced with another. I would never condone that, but the work his mother has done growing limbs, wings... Imagine if we could provide that level of healing to everyone."

All good things started out with the best of intentions. "It's playing God."

"Or it's evolution."

"Evolution is supposed to happen on its own."

"And it is. Mankind has gone from a primitive living in the dirt to sophisticated enough to create tools to build things. Medicine isn't really any different. It's evolved with us."

"Mastermind's and Mother Q's research comes at the expense of others."

"Which is why we should try and at least see if some of it can be used for good."

"Good?" She snorted. "How can it be good to know how to change someone from a kangaroo to a bear?"

"Actually, in the case of those dealing with identity issues, it might be a cure. Look at Mastermind. She only ever wanted to be a different animal."

"Jakob doesn't though."

"And that is unfortunate. Perhaps, once he's gotten used to his new shape, he'll appreciate it. Pandas are rare and valued. Did you know they are the only kind of shifter allowed to counsel the emperor?"

"Do you really think Jakob is advisor material?" He'd probably start a world war just to play with toys that went boom.

"No, but if we figure out how it was done, perhaps we can change him again. Change all those that never felt right in their skin. As if they were meant to be someone else."

"Humans, too?" she asked.

"That decision wouldn't be up to me."

"But you don't think it's a bad idea," she blurted out in a moment of perception.

"Right now, there are many more of them than us. We could even those odds."

"By changing them into shifters? How does that make us any better than the Masterminds of this world?"

"I made a vow to save lives, meaning if we don't act

and the humans turn against us, how many will die?" Nolan spread his hands. "Too many."

"Why does everyone assume mass extinction? We've been coexisting forever. Nothing has to change." She said it and yet wondered if she truly believed it. They lived in polarized times where social media exacerbated issues.

"What if you're wrong? Shouldn't we have a backup plan in place so we don't end up in cages, or worse?"

She eyed the vials of blood. She could get rid of them. It wouldn't be hard to crush them under her foot.

But she'd brought them for a reason. Answers. Could she predict what would happen if they unraveled the truth? No. Would she let the fear of the unknown stop her?

"Let's get started."

They didn't make any epic discoveries over the next few hours as they partitioned the samples out and set them up for various tests. Given the hour grew late, she returned to the guesthouse ready for some sleep while the machines ran their course. She held the rail as she trudged up the stairs to her room. She ran into Jakob on her way. And by running into him, she meant she knocked on his door until he answered, bleary eyed and shirtless.

"Maze? Everything okay?"

"No." She pushed past him and entered his room to pace. "I don't know if bringing you here was a good idea."

"Actually, it was a great one. I'm already doing much better." Said by a man with two black eyes. Given how green they looked, they must have been doozies to have not healed already.

"You don't understand. They want to use you for tests. See how your mom changed you."

"Awesome."

"No, it's not awesome."

He frowned. "Don't you want me to get fixed?"

"Of course I do. It's just…" She huffed out a hard breath. "What if that information falls into the wrong hands? What if someone figures out what was done to you and starts changing folks?"

"Most people aren't like my mother."

"Most. Not all. There are some who would sell that knowledge to someone unscrupulous."

"Yep, there are some who would."

"What if it's better we don't find out?"

"What if. What if. It's a game that can go on forever. I should know. I used to play that game a lot. Still do. Like what if I'd fought harder to win you back?"

"What if you'd chosen me and never left at all?" At his expression, she immediately felt contrite.

"You know I did that for my family."

"I thought I was your family."

"I will say it again, I was stupid. Can you ever forgive me?"

"Why do you care if I do?" she asked, noting the intensity of his expression.

"Because how else can I get another chance?"

"To what?"

"What do you think, Maze? I never stopped loving you."

He'd said it. First. Out loud. And her heart raced in reply. "Things have changed. I'm not the same person I was."

"Me either. Which is why I'm hoping you'll give me a second go. I promise, things will be different."

She shook her head. "It's not just me I have to think about. There's Peach, too."

"Give me a chance to prove myself. Please."

She eyed him, uncertain. Had he been cocky, she might have had a different reply. But the vulnerability in his tone made the decision for her.

She grabbed him by the cheeks and kissed him. Pressed her mouth hard against his and felt him stiffen. He froze as if unsure how to act.

So she told him, "This is where you kiss me back."

"Maze." Her name was but a rumble, and it made her shiver down to her toes.

Drawn into his room, with the door shut, they did an awkward shuffle walk toward the bed, made more difficult because she latched onto his neck, sucking the slightly bristly skin, loving the lingering soapy flavor and inhaling his scent. She nibbled at the flesh, and he stumbled. Kind of gratifying to know she had that effect on him.

She pulled away far enough that she could shove him. His legs hit the bed, and he fell over. She pounced and crawled up his body, blowing against his naked torso, chuckling as he clenched the comforter rather than manhandle her like he obviously desired.

She crawled high enough that she could reach his lips, dipping to plaster her mouth over his, the passion of their embrace stealing her breath. But she didn't need words for him to grasp her impatience.

His hands pulled at her top, and she helped him to remove it, delighting in the feel of his fingers over the skin of her back. Her breasts, still clad in her bra, brushed against his bare chest. Her nipples hardened behind the fabric.

She lifted herself far enough that she could dangle them as an offering for his mouth. He latched on, his mouth tugging and sucking at the erect tip, soaking the cup of her bra, making her shiver and quiver between her legs.

With a twist of her body, she swapped breasts and moaned as he treated the other side to the same attention, each sharp tug a zing to her pussy.

She ground against him, delighting in the hardness of his erection against her sex. She leaned up and braced her hands on his defined chest. She ran her fingers over the flesh of his torso, tracing the muscles under the layer of softness, noticing they had thickened since the last time she touched him.

He sucked in a breath as her hands slid over the ripples of his abs. She dragged her nails down his sensitive underbelly, following the ridge that disappeared into his trackpants.

There were too many layers separating them. She tugged his pants down over his hips, wiggling backwards as she maneuvered them out of the way.

He wore no underwear. His cock sprang to attention the moment she freed it. She eyed that long shaft as she finished denuding him then made him wait a moment longer as she stripped the rest of her clothes, too.

Standing at the foot of the bed, she licked her lips.

"Waiting for something?" he asked in a low voice.

"Debating actually. Do I suck you and then ride you? Or do I make you lick me and then ride you? Or do I just ride you?"

He moaned, and his cock twitched.

She grinned. Nice having all the power, which was why she knelt between his legs and grabbed hold of his velvety shaft. The heat of the flesh just about scorched as she wrapped her fingers around him. It pulsed at her touch, a long, living thing capable of such pleasure.

She squeezed her thighs as the anticipation made her quiver.

She blew lightly on him, and his cock jerked. Actually, his whole body shook. She cast him a sloe-eyed peek and was gratified to see him staring at her, his eyes smoldering with passion. Holding his gaze, she stuck her tongue out and lapped at his full head, the salty pearl at the tip the right place to start her licking. She swirled her tongue down the length of him, along the ridge. He moaned as she lapped at him. He fisted the comforter as she inhaled him into her mouth and sucked.

His hips bucked, and his fingers threaded her hair as she began to bob his shaft, sliding her mouth up and down the length of him. His rock-solid flesh pulsed in her mouth. She grazed him with her teeth, and he gasped. She pinched the tip harder, and his hips thrust so hard she had to hold on.

He groaned and bucked as she sucked him harder, trying to make him come, but he held off, groaning and fighting.

"Come for me," she whispered.

"Not until I'm balls deep," was his reply before he changed his grip to grab her and pull her up the length of his body until he could kiss her.

He rolled her onto her back and embraced her hard, his tongue sliding along hers, his body heavy against her. His hands roamed, sliding under her frame, grasping her ass cheeks and squeezing. He yanked her against him, pinning his erect cock between their bodies, grinding against her clit, making her gasp. Pant. Ache.

She wiggled until his cock ended up where she wanted it, pressed against the opening of her sex. Her legs wrapped around his waist. It took only tightening them to pull him into her, the thickness of his shaft stretching her nicely. When he'd gotten as deep as he could go, he paused and she was the one to pulse, her pussy tightening around him. Wanting…

"Oh."

He pulled out and slowly slid in.

Out.

In.

A slow torturous tease that had her digging her nails into his back.

"Give it to me," she huffed, aching for satisfaction.

He growled in reply and slammed his cock home. A cry emerged from her, a noise of satisfaction that was almost a humming purr as he pumped her. He filled her so perfectly. Gave her plenty to clench. Their mouths remained meshed, their kiss passionate and hot with panting breath.

Her nails dug in as her body raced toward a pinnacle of pleasure. He pounded faster, the angle hitting her just right, just….

"Ahhhhh!" She couldn't help but scream as she climaxed, her body bowing and taut as the bliss rolled over her.

He kept going, pistoning into her faster. A firm grip on her hips, he thrust even harder into her, the bumping action reviving her orgasm and rolling her into a second one. This time he came with her. Yelling her name. Spilling against her womb. Collapsing atop her, his weight welcome.

The smell of blood, though… She glanced over his shoulder to see she'd partially shredded his back.

"Oh shoot. I'm sorry," she gasped, ready to run for a medical kit.

But the smug man rolled to her side, tucked her into a spoon against him, and rumbled, "Sorry about what? I'll wear those marks as a badge of honor."

"Everyone will think I've claimed you."

"They wouldn't be wrong," was his reply.

12

HE'D SPILLED HIS HEART. Told her what he felt. What he hoped for.

And did she suddenly succumb and declare her undying love?

No. But she did have sex with him. Epic, mind-blowing, beat-his-chest sex that had him passed out hard after —hopefully not snoring. When he woke, he found her snuggled against him. Where she belonged.

Problem was she hadn't come around to his way of thinking yet. Which he could understand. He'd hurt her. Caused her to lose faith in him. Made her believe she wasn't the most important thing in his life. At the time, she might have been right. After all, he'd chosen his family over his relationship.

And had regretted it ever since.

If he wanted to make a go with Maisy, he'd have to be able to commit wholeheartedly. No more secrets. No more choosing anyone over her. Time to show her he was a changed man.

That didn't prove easy. During the day, they barely saw

or spoke. The things they had him busy doing made the hours pass in a blur.

He had lessons in how to be a bear. It wasn't all picnic baskets and eating honey. The way a bear moved was drastically different than a kangaroo. The weight dispersed in ratios that meant relearning how his limbs worked.

When he wasn't figuring out how to walk on two legs in his new shape, he sparred, discovering great strength in his blows—when he managed to land them. He didn't have the same speed as before.

When he wasn't training, he volunteered to be a hamster in a lab—where he got to see Maze. Sort of. She worked on the samples with all kinds of expensive machinery, whereas he spent most of his time in the patient areas, donating blood and providing tissue samples. He even ran on a treadmill with wires hooked to him. All in the name of science—and peeks at the woman who was rocking his nights.

Every morning she snuck out of his bed as if he were a dirty secret. All day long he'd wonder if she regretted it, and then, that night, they would look at each other over dinner, or they'd run into each other coming back to the guesthouse. Within moments they'd find a room, his, hers, didn't matter. The evening always ended up naked and satisfying. And if they woke at the same time in the middle of the night, the bed was solid enough not to make noise and wake any of the other guests.

Over the course of that week, Jakob found a new equilibrium. He'd moved past needing strong emotion to trigger a shift and had been practicing slipping in and out of his panda. While he did not yet feel at complete ease in his skin, he'd at least progressed to comfortable. He didn't trip on his own paws anymore, and when he swung, he now connected, even harder than before now that he had some weight behind it.

Given he didn't have the bouncy hind legs, he sought out new moves. He studied a few movies, including the famous *Kung Fu Panda*. Sure, the cartoon aspect exaggerated the possibilities. For example, he couldn't leap and hang suspended in the air. Gravity worked doubly quickly on his weight it seemed, and he fell rapidly each time. But he could body slam hard enough to make the earth shake.

Despite the hind kick being his favorite move as a roo, he couldn't manage even a partial foot lunge without falling over. On the flip side, with his grippy paws, he could climb. Trees. Buildings. He could scale anything he could sink claws into, which he had to admit was kind of cool, especially when he climbed to Maisy's window after a particularly long day and tapped on the glass.

He knew she was in there. Had seen her shadow passing by the curtain, but she didn't answer his knock. He plastered his face to the glass. "Grawr." He couldn't exactly say her name.

She heard and turned, blinking at him before sliding up the sash. He slipped in before shifting.

"Was it too complicated to come in through the front and knock?" she asked.

"Don't be jealous just because I'm a master climber."

That brought an unladylike snort to her lips. "You're mediocre at best."

Which was better than useless. "You look worried. Have you still not managed to reach your dad?" She'd talked to him only twice since their arrival.

She shook her head. "He's not answering any of the numbers I have for him."

"I thought he left you a message yesterday."

"He did. Two words. Doing great, according to him."

"You think your dad is lying?"

"I think it's odd he's not answering or that I haven't heard from Peach since we left," she said with a scowl.

"Surely he'd tell you if something happened."

Judging by her expression, maybe not. "Want me to sic my brothers on his trail?"

"They're already looking. Jebbie hasn't been able to find any traces of him."

He tried to not be jealous at her nickname for his brother. Jeb had known her longer, but Jakob had seen her naked. "Meaning he's hiding real good."

"Or he's been taken, and Peach with him, and the messages I'm getting are fake and meant to keep me from looking."

Her worry was contagious. "When do we leave?"

"Who said I was leaving?"

He eyed the bag with clothes spilling out of it. "Were you just going to hare off without saying anything?"

Her shoulders slumped. "This is my problem, not yours."

"I call dingo shit. If you're worried, then I'm worried. I like Peach and your dad. So let's put our minds at ease and book a flight home."

"You can't go. You're still learning."

"Bah. I'm fine."

She arched a brow. "Is that why you're here instead of doing your agility exercises with Georgina?"

His lip jutted. "She wants to pit my skills against the simians in her development department."

"And?"

"Those monkeys cheat. They always win because they

can use their tails," he grumbled. "Plus, they steal my bamboo."

"Poor bear," she mock-soothed.

"That's right, poor me. I need a hug."

"Only a hug?" she teased, coming close.

"And maybe a kiss to make me feel better."

"Just a single one?" she said before pressing her mouth to his.

Her heat enflamed all his senses. His hands reached to cup her ass and yank her close to him.

It might have gotten inappropriate really fast if a little voice hadn't said, "Why are you kissing my mommy?"

Jakob froze and slid his hands to Maisy's hips, mostly to ensure she didn't move, given he was naked and hard, but shriveling quickly due to their audience.

"Peach?" A surprised Maisy turned to look to her left and the tousled head that suddenly popped up from the pillows.

"Hi, Mommy!" The little girl beamed and waved.

"How did you get here?" Maze sputtered.

A good question, because until that child showed herself, he didn't have an inkling she was there. Her scent hadn't even triggered, yet now her vibrant youth filled the room.

Odd.

"I took a plane," Peach declared.

"With Pappy?"

The child shook her head. "He said no. Pappy wanted us to hide, but you need me."

"Did you have one of your visions?" Maze asked softly, turning to face her daughter.

Jakob used the cover of her back to reach for a robe

lying over a chair. It wouldn't fit quite right, but it beat standing in the buff.

"The bad people are coming for me."

"Like hell they are," Jakob stated, tying the sash. Didn't take a leap to know Peach meant his mother. "I'm going to make sure all the bad people stay far away from you." He'd die before he let anyone harm the little girl.

Maze appeared somewhat shell-shocked. "How did you get into the Academy? Who let you in?"

Meaning, who hadn't notified Maisy her daughter had arrived? And how was it neither of them perceived her scent until she announced her presence?

"I snuck in. It wasn't very hard. The slow man never even saw me," Peach stated, beaming with pride.

Maisy, however, looked fit to explode. "Of all the dangerous, irresponsible things. You mean to tell me you left Pappy, hiked to the nearest town—"

"I didn't walk long. A nice man in a big truck gave me a ride."

Maisy's eyes almost fell out of her head. "Made your way to the city with a stranger, boarded a plane—"

"Inside a suitcase once I took out the clothes. But I kept the snacks."

"Then what? Hitchhiked to the Academy?"

"Yes," Peach replied.

Jakob could see Maze held on only by the barest of threads so he stepped in to give her a chance to compose herself. "Are you okay? No one tried to hurt you?"

Those big brown eyes turned on him, and the little girl's smile melted his insides. "I know how to hide."

"I think you scared your mother, though."

"Try more like I'm pissed. I want to know why my dad

didn't admit what had happened. Going great my butt!" Maze ranted. "I am going to kill him."

The bedroom door suddenly opened. "Don't blame me because she's good. I had a hell of a time following our girl." Herbert walked in with beetled brows. "You!" He pointed to Peach.

Jakob tensed, ready to intervene if the old guy did something.

"Hi, Pappy!"

Herbert beamed. "Excellent work. I barely managed to track you."

"You mean you were following her the entire time and didn't stop her?" Maisy said softly. Too softly.

Perhaps Jakob should step back before she drew blood and stained the fluffy white robe.

Her father looked a tad nervous. "She was never in any real danger."

"You let her smuggle herself on a plane in the cargo area."

"With snacks," Herbert added. "Better than what they were serving on board, I'll add."

Maisy flung her hands. "I can't believe you're here. I thought you were hiding. You should have been safe in one of your hidey holes."

The child emerged from under the covers and bounced close enough she could pat her mother on the arm. "No one is safe, Mommy. The badness is coming."

"Unless we stop it first." Jakob should have thought it odd a child was prophesying, and yet, her words matched the nagging in his gut.

Something wicked this way came. Best be prepared.

Herbert caught them up on more details of Peach's cross-continent and ocean adventure while Maze cradled her daughter in her lap. Then Herbert left, looking for food and some open space. Days of confined travelling had left him grumpy.

He might have also wanted to leave before Maze tore him into strips. Despite Peach's obvious good health and humor, the mama panther in her bristled at the danger her cub had weathered.

Once Herbert left, Maze eyed Peach. "What am I going to do with you?"

"Love me." The child batted her lashes, and Jakob was ready to kneel down and promise his devotion.

Her mother didn't melt. "You disobeyed my orders."

"You need me."

"I need you to be safe," Maze barked, and tears brimmed in Peach's eyes.

Jakob knew he shouldn't, but he threw himself into the fray. "She's probably safer at the Academy."

"Now, but what about the days spent travelling here? Do you know what could have happened?" Her voice cracked.

Peach sniffled as she held out her arms. "I'm sorry, Mommy."

"Oh, my little fuzz." They wrapped each other in a hug, Maisy crushing her cub tight as a bear and nuzzling her head. "You are much too clever."

"And wily. I think Peach needs to teach me how she hides," Jakob exclaimed.

"You're too big!" Peach declared with a giggle.

"It's my butt, isn't it?" He glanced behind, and the child laughed again before holding out her arms.

Jakob hesitated only a half-second before reaching for her. She clambered into his arms, and he got treated to a hug, too. A nice hug, the kind that had Maisy staring at him softly with a smile.

Was she also picturing what it would be like if they were a family?

He got a taste of what that meant as Peach chose the middle of the bed as her spot. Maisy climbed in beside her, and when he would have left, Peach grumbled, "You sleep there." She pointed to the empty space on her other side.

It was a crowded affair, with Pappy thankfully choosing to camp outside in the forest. But Jakob wouldn't have given it up for anything.

Not even the part where he woke up to a tiger cub gnawing on his nose.

He gave Peach a lazy swat that tumbled her over. She returned to perch on his chest and dug her claws in and uttered a soft grumble. Being a man, and one of five brothers, he knew of only one recourse. He flipped the sheet and farted.

The cub's eyes widened, but it was the drawled, "Good morning to you, too," that heated his cheeks.

He glanced over to see an amused Maisy. "Um, sorry?"

"It's a good thing I have almost no sense of smell," she muttered as she rolled out of bed. She didn't even stagger as an energetic bundle of striped fur launched itself at her. She tucked the squirming Peach under her arm. "I'm going to take her outside for a run before breakfast."

"Want company?"

"Why don't you sleep in a bit longer. I'll probably run into Miranda and Kelly. They usually pass by every fifteen minutes in the morning until Chase gets up around nine."

He watched them go and smiled.

His girls.

Holy bamboo stick dipped in chocolate. *His* girls. Being

with them made him so happy. This was what had been missing in his life. A family of his own.

Now to convince Maisy to make the situation permanent.

He fell back asleep, mostly because he could. His morning class with Everett—he of the finely tuned nose—was cancelled. Something about the start of deer season setting off his wife.

He might have slept all day if there wasn't a banging at his door. The kind of knocking that screamed panic.

He rolled out of bed and stumbled to the door to fling it open. Chase, his hair untidy and tie askew, paced outside.

Cold dread immediately gripped him. "What happened?"

"They're gone."

"Who's gone?" he asked, his stomach sinking. It occurred to him no one had ever returned to the room.

"All of them," grumbled the bear, whose skin rippled in agitation. "They took my honeys and yours, too."

"Shit." Understatement. "How? Was the Academy attacked?"

"The girls went to the mall to buy some stuff for Peach. They should have been okay. They had Tom along for support. But it's as if their kidnappers knew they were going and set up ahead of time." Chase paced the hall.

"Wait, you mean to say Miranda, Maze, Peach, and Kelly have all been taken?"

"Tom, too. I told you, whoever it was came prepared. I am going to eat their faces," Chase growled.

"I'll help you to eat them, but first we have to find the bastards."

"We've already got a team of FUC agents on their trail.

They wouldn't take me. Said they were worried I'd go grizzly or something in public." Spoken with a hint of fang and fur.

"Will you?"

"Most definitely. They took my honeys." Which sounded like a perfectly reasonable answer to Jakob. He was feeling kind of rumbly himself.

"We have to get them back."

"I would if we could find them. The van they tossed them in was stolen and abandoned a mile away from the mall."

"Any clues in it?"

"No." Chase tucked his hands behind his back. "They set it on fire before they abandoned it."

"Do we have a description of their kidnappers?"

Again, Chase shook his head. "Just some crappy video footage."

"Can I see?"

Jakob watched the attack in the store several times. The way the kidnappers surprised both Miranda and Maisy, as if the women never smelled them coming. But it was the faces of two of them that made him realize who was behind it.

"This was my mother's doing." Once more, she'd sent her thugs to sedate and abduct, but this time, she'd gone too far. Kidnapping children, a pregnant woman, and his Maisy.

She must be getting desperate or arrogant to strike so boldly. Worse, they probably didn't have much time before she did something to them. If she was willing to change her own son, then there wasn't anything she wouldn't do.

"You said it seemed like they knew where to find our girls. Does the Academy have a traitor?"

Chase's expression turned grim. "If we do, I'll eat them."

"First we have to figure out who it is."

"How? We don't have time to waste."

A good point. How to draw out the traitor and use them to track down his mother?

The idea hit him like a left hook from his brother Jackson. "I have an idea."

They were still arguing as they entered the main building.

"The Academy is on lockdown. How many times do I have to say no one in or out?" Chase bellowed.

"I'm not a kid. You cannot tell me what to do," Jakob hollered back, planting himself in the Academy's entrance. They had an audience, but that didn't stop his fight with Chase.

"You're a student here."

"Consider this me dropping out."

"If you go, you won't be allowed back," Chase threatened as Jakob walked out the door.

"Fine!"

"Fine!" Chase echoed.

Jakob had the guy in the security booth at the gate call him a taxi, the same guy in the green suit that had been manning it when he arrived. Could he be the one telling the enemy their movements?

He sent Chase a text. The taxi first took him to the mall where Maisy was taken. Jakob walked the length of it before entering the store that hadn't yet closed for the night. He could see the salesperson eyeballing him, probably pegging him for a pedophile given how he kept sniffing around the racks. Before she could call the cops, he left and made his way to where the vehicle that had transported them was abandoned and burned. The frame of it had already been removed, leaving behind only a scorch march. He knelt by it and ran his fingers through the greasy remains on the ground.

Then off he went to get drunk at the nearest bar he could find. It wasn't exactly his style with its flashing techno colors and pulsating beat, but the tequila was good, especially when chugged by the bottle. He sent a few messages, telling people where he was in case they heard anything. Even sent one to the guy at the gate warning him he'd be back late.

As they neared closing time, he sat slumped on the bar, no closer to finding Maisy and Peach, piles of empty glasses in front of him, wondering if he'd miscalculated his worth. He could have sworn eyes had followed him as he retraced Maze and Peach's steps. Thought for sure he'd—

Even through the miasma of tequila wafting from his shirt where he'd spilled it, he smelled her. He peeled open an eye and managed a not-too-slurred, "Hallo, Mummy."

13

BACKDOOR FUC

In a nearby van with blacked-out windows…

"They took the bait!" Everett announced, throwing his hands in the air. The wolf shifter, former FUC agent, and former PI had taken a temporary teaching position at the Academy with his pregnant wife. Teaching in a classroom wasn't his forte. He much preferred being out in the field, playing with gadgets, outsmarting folks, and getting the goods.

Like now. The small microphone pinned inside Jakob's shirt let them hear everything being said. Through it, they heard Mother Q snap, "Pulse him just in case he's carrying a bug."

Bzzt. The microphone went dead, but they'd expected that possibility.

The backup drone sat atop an electrical pole outside and had its camera trained on the entrance to the bar. Everett and Chase watched via a drone feed as Mother Q led a very drunk Jakob out of the bar. Everett tapped on his keyboard, sending a message to the strike team.

They had a plan, concocted by Jakob, and then implemented as quickly as they could. It wasn't quick enough for a certain bear.

"Screw waiting. Let's go get my honeys!" Chase slammed his fist into his palm.

Having worked for years as a PI, Everett knew better than to rush in. "Patience, my friend. Stick to the plan. We can't rush in. Not until Mother Q leads us to her secret lair."

"It's taking too long," Chase grumbled. "I still say my idea was better."

The usually calm and measured bear had suggested nabbing Mother Q and torturing her for information. Everett might not approve of the woman, but he did have some lines he wouldn't cross.

"Abducting her is hasty. What if she triggers an alarm that does something to her prisoners? If we don't know where they are, we might not arrive in time."

"I hate waiting!" Chase was barely coherent, worry for his mate and child making him lose his grip on his beast.

"Waiting sucks," Everett agreed. "But it shouldn't be much longer now." He pointed to the screen. "Mother Q took Jakob."

"And? What if she doesn't take him to the same place as my honeys?"

That was the one major flaw in their plan. They couldn't be sure what Mother Q would do, yet they had no other option. If she didn't lead them to the right place, then they might have to explore Chase's more violent idea.

"We'll find them," Everett replied. They had to because he knew Miranda and little Kelly. Too energetic by far, but good people. Everyone at the Academy was the very best, and this was where he and Dawn would have their first child. It was something that had to be protected.

"Where is the strike team?" Chase muttered.

"They're on their way." Everett pointed to an incoming transmission. "ETA less than fifteen minutes."

"Too long."

"We've almost got them, my friend. So sit down, dive into that box of honey cruller donuts, and in no time at all, the strike team will be taking Mother Q into custody and freeing everyone she's taken captive."

"Your optimism is annoying."

"Would it help if I said I am planning a severe beating to anyone who dares harm Miranda and Kelly?"

"I'll eat them," Chase exclaimed with a hint of muzzle and fang.

"Check this out." Everett pointed to a blinking blip on the screen. A tracker, embedded inside Jakob, built to withstand most handheld electrical disruptors. It gave out a steady signal they could follow. "Looks like they're heading our way. Shall we parallel their route?" Everett asked, swiveling in his seat.

"I'm driving." Chase didn't wait for assent as he rocked through the van, heading for the front.

"Sounds like a plan. Let me send the signal to our dashboard GPS." A few swipes of his mouse and their route was being calculated to stay within a mile of their subject. It wouldn't do to be spotted.

Mother Q and her henchmen didn't try to obfuscate their path. They drove straight to a small airstrip with a single hangar. A helicopter sat on the runway, blades whirring, prepped to leave.

"Shit. They're taking a chopper," Chase stated, taking his eyes off the road to stare past the chain-link fence as they drove by.

"We don't know that for sure," Everett said, even as

Mother Q's car drove right up to the heli and stopped, spilling its occupants.

"They're getting away!" Chase yelled, slamming his foot down on the gas hard enough that the van swerved.

"Don't go berserk," Everett yelled, hands braced on the dash.

But Chase—more bear than man in that moment—seethed. His big hairy hands gripped the steering wheel so tight it twisted.

"Slow down."

Rather than brake to take the corner, Chase spun the vehicle and sent them careening on two wheels.

Everett closed his eyes and didn't open them again until the thump indicated they'd settled back on pavement and not upside down.

What he saw had him exclaiming, "Don't ram it!"

"They can't leave." The words were barely recognizable amidst the gruff.

Everett once more closed his eyes and braced for impact while hoping that FUC hadn't skimped on the extras. Let there be airbags.

Whup. Whup. He could hear the spinning of the blades over the whine of the engine.

Any second now. Any—

Screech. He was tossed around as a vigorous brake saw them slowing rapidly and spinning. When they stopped moving, he saw the blinking lights of a helicopter lifting into the sky.

"Too late!" Chase slammed the steering wheel, which finally collapsed from the abuse.

"Don't give up yet."

Grabbing his phone, Everett dialed a secure line.

It rang once and then clicked, but no one said anything.

"Strike Team Bounce, this is Howling Mobile HQ. Target has just departed in a helicopter. Will attempt to follow from the ground."

"Don't worry, HMHQ. We are already on their tail. I've got it from here," announced the strike team commander.

Everett hung up and reached over to pat Chase, who was slumped, his head pressed to the wrecked steering wheel.

"I broke our ride. We have no way of getting there," Chase moaned.

"Says who?" Emmett pulled out a tablet. "I requested this van for a reason. It's been modified to be able to handle nondrivers." He held out his device. "Auto pilot." The van shifted into motion, and Chase lifted his head.

"You mean…"

"We are going to find your honeys."

MEANWHILE, BACK AT THE ACADEMY, THE DRAMA WAS unfolding for a trusted roomful. They watched as the strike team fed a live video of their arrival, their bodies rappelling out of the helicopter. Some not going far, just the rooftop of the building where they infiltrated from above. Others went to ground, crouched and moving off in a preplanned synchronization.

When the explosives went off, creating a giant hole in the wall of the modern building, the watching shifters cheered!

"FUC! FUC! FUC!"

"FUC is gonna give it to them."

"All for FUC, FUC for all."

"Why is it everyone neglects ASS?" shouted an irritated voice.

The chattering tapered off as smoke and dust particles obscured the video feed, but they could hear gunfire and yelling, the violence of it chilling.

The room full of cryptids then did something very human. They prayed.

14

MAISY WOKE in a cage and did her best to not panic. That proved harder than expected when she realized Peach wasn't with her. Her first impulse? Run for the bars and grab them.

Zap. The jolt of electricity sent her flying, and she hit the floor hard on her ass. She lay there and groaned, waiting for her body to stop tingling.

She didn't need to touch her hair to know it currently stood in a wild halo from her head, an effect she'd spent hours trying to achieve. The next time she needed to do her hair, she'd have to try sticking her finger in a socket. If there was a next time…

She sat up and, rather than rush the bars, tried to pay attention to what was around her.

Cages, for starters. Eight she counted, and only two without an occupant. Miranda was in the one directly across from her, lying on her side, a hand cradling her belly, her eyes closed.

And then they weren't.

Wide green eyes stared, and Miranda's mouth opened with a screeched, "Oh heck no!"

The tiny blonde woman vaulted to her feet, but before she could make the same mistake, Maisy hollered, "Don't touch the bars! They're electrified."

The warning halted Miranda. Seething through her nostrils, Miranda stood in front of them, fists clenched, expression wild. "Where's my Kelly?"

"I don't know. Peach is missing, too." She stood and noticed some of the other occupants eyeing them. Except for the sleeping man in the next cell over. Tom snorted away on the floor.

"This is humiliating," Miranda declared. "Captured like some simple forest creature. Ugh."

Maisy's jaw hitched as she recalled how oblivious she and Miranda had been to the danger.

For some reason, she'd thought herself safe, the incident at the airport more than a week old. Mother Q a continent away. And Maisy had no enemies. She'd agreed to go shopping and found herself in a children's clothing store, the most benign of places. Peach, being Peach, raced in and out of the racks with an accomplice for once. Little Kelly, who was only a year younger, chortled as she kept up with her, their laughter a clarion that signaled their location.

She and Miranda kept an eye out as they browsed clothes. Peach would need some things if she was sticking around, which seemed most likely. Jakob had a point. Sending her back would just expose her to danger. Might as well have her close by.

They weren't alone in the store. A handful of other women shopped, and in retrospect, Maisy should have wondered that not one had a child with her. It didn't help her feeble sense of smell never caught a hint of anything untoward. She felt at ease knowing they had Tom loitering just outside the entrance.

Miranda certainly didn't seem nervous. So when Maisy heard her daughter squeak, her first thought wasn't danger. Until she saw Peach dangling from the grip of a lady who mouthed, "Don't move."

Seeing the giant needle pressed against Peach's skin, she froze. Kelly didn't.

"No. No hurt my friend." The little girl slammed into the stranger holding Peach, and the needle went in. Peach's eyes widened in panic, and then she was a bundle of striped fur, snarling and snapping.

The woman holding her cursed and dropped Peach, who hit the floor on four paws. The cub hissed and swiped at a leg.

"Run, Peach!"

For a moment, she thought her daughter would keep trying to fight, but she obeyed and ran. Kelly went to follow, but the stranger acted fast, yanking a net from her pocket and dropping it over the child, tangling her limbs.

As Maisy ran to help, she heard Miranda snarl, "Get your hands away from my honey baby, or I will tear your head off and shove it where the sun don't shine!"

Doubtful, given Miranda couldn't shift while pregnant. But Maisy could. Problem was, there was a very human salesperson watching the unfolding drama. She already had a phone to her ear, meaning Maisy had to act fast.

Before she could reach Kelly, a striped bundle flew out of the clothes and hit the needle-wielding woman, knocking her over, but that was only one down. The others in the store were all moving toward Maisy and the kids. Poor Kelly still struggled to free herself from the net, and

Peach, a four-legged tiger cub, wavered on her feet as the drug took effect.

A quick glance back showed Miranda grappling with another assailant and having a hard time getting a grip with her pregnant belly in the way.

Maisy moved to help her, digging her hand into a pocket and emerging with a sachet of powder. She spilled some into her palm and moved behind Miranda's assailant, slapping her hand over the woman's mouth and nose. The assailant shut her mouth, knowing better than to inhale any of the dust; however, the need to breathe eventually proved too strong. The woman's lips parted to suck for air, even as her nostrils flexed. Only then did Maisy remove her hand, no need for it anymore, given her target choked and sputtered as she spun away from her.

Miranda grabbed hold of her as she dashed past. "The girls!"

Turning to follow, she saw the other two women moving in on the children, Kelly standing guard over her sleeping friend, her teeth looking longer and her tufted ears peeping through her hair.

Which was when Tom chose to enter, hands tucked behind his back. "Excuse me, ladies."

The first one to turn and look got a taser to the chest. She hit the ground, but the other one ignored the threat Tom posed and grabbed Kelly in a headlock.

Miranda uttered a primal scream that sent the human salesgirl ducking behind the counter.

The woman holding Kelly smirked. "Yell all you like. I have your child, and if you want her to live, then place your hands behind your head and come with us quietly."

With a glare that promised death, Miranda sank to her

knees, hands laced behind her head, and Maisy followed suit. Surely, they would find a way out of this.

She wanted to hold on to that hope, but as a needle approached her, all she could think of was what had happened to Jakob. Would she wake up as someone else?

Staring at Peach, being held by a stranger, in danger, she could only bow her head.

Which was why she'd woken up in a cell with Peach gone.

Maisy hunched and sighed. "This is bad."

"Don't look so blue."

"How can I not be depressed? We're the prisoners of a mad woman."

Miranda had lost her enraged mien for a pensive one. "Would you believe this has happened to me before?"

"I heard."

Apparently, Miranda had decimated a Mastermind installation. Rumor had it she'd ripped off some arms and used them as weapons. Probably an exaggeration.

"Let's turn that frown upside down. Never fear. My honey bear will come to the rescue."

"How?" Maisy asked. "He has no idea where we are."

"As if that will stop him." Miranda winked. "My honey won't let his girls down."

It made her wonder what Jakob would do.

She got her answer a moment later as the elevators at the far end of the holding room opened and a gurney was wheeled out. As it passed, she gasped because, strapped to it, reeking of booze, with his eyes closed and his mouth slack, was Jakob. Idiot must have gotten drunk and let down his guard.

Mother Q had acquired yet another victim and provided another reminder that family meant nothing to her. Where did children fall on the scale? Maisy feared the answer.

Only once the thugs left with Jakob dumped into a cell did she hiss at Miranda. "We need to get out of these cages and find our girls."

"I agree."

"So, how do we do it?"

"We don't." And that bunny, that crazy rascally rabbit, beamed as she looked overhead and, in a voice eerily reminiscent of a certain eighties horror movie, sang, "They're here."

15

PLAYING the part of sleeping man proved easier than expected. Snore, drool, and fart. An act that served to convince those who captured Jakob that he'd succumbed to their drugs. What they didn't know was he'd activated a slow-release adrenaline pill embedded under his skin the moment he saw his mother. It helped to counter the sedative effect.

Although he did allow himself a short nap on the helicopter. And during the car ride to the secret lair. Even once he got to his cage, he knew better than to act too quickly, even though excitement filled him as he caught a certain scent.

He'd found Maze, but he couldn't smell Peach. What had happened to the sweet little girl? His mother better not have harmed her!

One problem at a time. He had to stick to the plan.

He waited to hear the distant rumble that indicated the expected explosives had been detonated before he acted, rising from the pallet he'd been tossed on, unrolling his sleeves to pull out the thin rubber gloves folded within.

Idiots never even stripped him. Good henchmen were so hard to find.

He slid to his knees in front of the cage door and glanced over at the other cells. He saw a snoring Tom and some other person, sleeping with knees tucked to their face. Beyond them, Maisy, who paced with her head down and hadn't yet realized he'd wakened. But Miranda had. She eyed him and his rubber gloves and the tube he pulled from inside his belt.

He was happy to see the cell had the basics like a prison, with a sink bolted to the wall and a toilet. Both of them were fused too tight to be knocked off, but that was where the tubing came into play. He stuck one end in the toilet, sucked on the other until the water just about reached his lips, and then yanked it free, letting it jet onto the floor. He aimed it toward the bars.

Water and electricity? Never a good combination.

Snap. Crackle. Pop. Even with rubber gloves, he felt a tingle.

Maisy finally noticed his antics. "Jakob, you're awake."

"Hey, Maze. You okay?"

"Better than you. How did they capture you?"

"Who says they did?" He winked as he stepped onto the edge of the toilet and balanced as the water kept spilling.

"What are you doing?"

"Getting us out of here, Maze. Where's Peach?"

"I don't know." Her voice wavered.

"Then the first thing we'll do once I bust us out is find her."

"And Kelly," Miranda added.

"Of course. Just give me a second to defuse the bars, and then I'll get to work popping the locks." Because this was the kind of stuff he excelled at. Difficult situations requiring special skills.

The lights flickered as the water did its trick and blew the breaker. The humming in the bars stopped. Only then did he reach into the buckle on his belt. The lockpicks slid into his hand. He'd counted on his mother not stripping him. Although, if she had, he had more tools stashed in his prison wallet. Something his ass was trying to forget.

It took him longer than he liked before the tumblers clicked. Too long. Those manning the cameras had surely sent guards to subdue him by now. Or were they too busy with the diversion upstairs? He could hear distant explosions that sounded worse than they were. Pros didn't kill those they were coming to rescue, but they did like to cause confusion.

And his family were pros at this kind of extraction. Part of his plan had entailed calling his brothers and telling big brother Jackson, *"Mum stole Maze and Peach, along with some other people. I want them back."*

"How can we help?" No hesitation on his brother's part.

"I'm going to tempt Mum into taking me and then want you guys to come in and save me." Because he'd finally figured out why she'd let him loose. She thought her experiment failed, and rather than kill him, she dumped him when he was of no use. But now that she knew he could shift again, he had a feeling she might be wanting her pet project back. Or so he hoped. But for his plan to work, he needed help. With Maisy and Peach in danger, he couldn't let pride get in his way.

Here was hoping they pulled it off.

The moment the lock clicked open on his cage also turned out to be the same moment the elevator opened and three guards spilled out. For the purpose of keeping them identified, he mentally named them Goons One, Two, and Three, with One sporting a unibrow, Two gripping two needles, and the third armed with a semi-automatic rifle.

Not the best odds. Jakob wouldn't have time to free anyone else before the guards were on him, so he began to strip.

Miranda yelled, "Yee haw. Someone give the guy a dollar."

She rattled her dead bars, drawing the eyes of the guards, which was perfect. It allowed Jakob time to shift and run. By the time goons one through three peeked at him, he was soaring, his big bear body creating quite the impact as it slammed into the closest guard. Something cracked as they went down. Goon Three with his gun didn't get back up.

Jakob rolled and bounced to his feet, stood on one leg and put his paws together, which confused Goon One and caused his caterpillar brow to contract. He raised a can of aerosol, and Jakob grunted before he hopped onto his other foot and hit himself in the stomach, "Oof."

Goon One hesitated while Goon Two inched around to his left.

He planted both hind paws and held his arms in an Egyptian pose, which only served to cause more confusion. Which was fine. It gave Tom, the slow-moving sloth who drew no attention, time to use the lockpicks Jakob had tossed into his cage as he'd gone by.

Now some people would wonder just what good a sloth was in a fight. They'd obviously never seen them in action. Sure, they moved slow, but when they swiped, watch out, those claws could be deadly.

The two guards were focused on Jakob, and cautious.

Jakob roared as he waddled—in a menacing fashion—at them. Goon Two darted at him and did his best to jab with his needle. The tip snapped off before he could push the plunger.

A chomp to the wrist ensured the screaming guard wouldn't try that again. Leaving Goon One and his pointed bottle, finger on the trigger.

Pssht. The idiot sprayed as he backed into Miranda's cage. She grabbed him by the head, rapped it off the bars, and shoved him at Jakob.

Jakob barreled into Goon One, knocking the guard down and then jumping until the limbs stopped twitching —which only took three bounces. By the time he turned around, Maze, Miranda, and the others were out of their cages.

The building shook as more stuff exploded. Jakob frowned at the sifting dust. "Something is wrong. My brothers wouldn't be trying to take this place down with us in it."

Maze's jaw tightened. "We need to find Peach."

The problem being the child had hidden her scent again, apparently something she could do at will. But while Peach could hid it, Kelly couldn't. Miranda took off like a rabbit chased by a hawk, or a mama whose instinct was screaming.

They ended up two levels above their prison floor in a hall lined with small two-by-two windows inset within doors and a strobing red light, but no sirens. Upon passing the first viewing window, Jakob slowed then stopped as he saw the horror within. A young face atop an eight-legged body. The room next to it showed a boy with four arms.

"She's got children here," he breathed. And she had experimented on them.

The entire floor was a warren of rooms, ten by ten, with a bed and a television and not much else. Jakob wanted to fling open every single door, and he would, but first he had something to do.

While Miranda ran, following the scent of her daughter, Jakob caught another smell. He galloped after it, only belatedly realizing Maze had chosen to follow him.

He weaved through the corridors until he reached one that resulted in a dead end. He slowed as he lumbered to the last door open just a crack, Maze by his side.

The mewl froze them both.

Maze dug her fingers into his fur. "Save my Peach."

He planned to.

The door swung open when he nudged it.

No surprise, his mother—dressed in crimson—sat on the bed, cradling a shivering cub.

"I underestimated you," stated Veronica.

Maze pushed past him. "Give me back my daughter."

"We both know she's not really your daughter." Mother Q snorted. "Not exactly, although ironically, we did take some strands from your line and a few from mine. The result was less than spectacular." She held Peach up by the scruff, which brought another plaintive mewl.

Jakob growled.

"Ah. Ah. Ah." His mum shook Peach, and all he could do was tremble in rage. "Don't take another step, or the child dies."

"Don't you threaten my daughter." Maze's tone oozed anger and fear.

"We both know she's not your daughter. You found her because she escaped one of my facilities. So perhaps I should thank you for returning my property."

Jakob seethed. How many times would his mother continue to hurt people?

Peach yawned and rolled her eyes. Could it be…did the little girl feign her trepidation?

Peach winked, and he suddenly had a plan. He shifted, dropping his hands to cover himself as he said, "Exactly how many children have you tried to create?"

"More than you can imagine. Unfortunately, a good number don't make it to their teens. Some modifications just aren't compatible. Take your half-brother for example. I knew better than to use Kole's genes, but he insisted. At least the girl child is showing some promise."

Cold. So damned cold. "No more." Jakob shook his head. "This has to stop."

"You're all afraid to act, and yet my way is the only way," his mother said with a tilt of her chin. "It is time we took back the power from the humans. That we became the dominant—Argh! You vicious little beast."

Mother Q had relaxed her grip on Peach as she ranted. Peach took advantage by twisting and chomping the hand that held her. The moment Mother Q let go, the cub ran for Jakob of all people, which turned out to be okay because Maze, the pacifist doctor, had finally gone feline.

The panther hit Veronica with a snarl, and given she managed to surprise, she got a good grip on her throat.

Jakob tucked Peach to his chest and stepped out of the room and across the hall while the battle raged. He didn't condemn what Maze did, but he wouldn't let the child see it.

He glanced into the viewing window of the room across the hall and stilled. There sat the girl from the press conference his mother had held. His half-sister.

He put his hand on the glass, and she raised her head

and snarled, her expression wild. He couldn't blame her. Raised in a prison.

"Fuzz!" Maze yelled.

"Mama!" Suddenly gangly limbs were shoving as Peach reached for her mother.

They hugged, the pair of them crying, and no, Jakob wasn't crying. It was just dusty in the hall.

Maze gave him a tearful gaze and mouthed, "Thank you." She held out an arm in invitation.

Jakob was about to join the love fest when Peach shouted, "Bad lady!"

"Oof." The sudden hug from behind squished his ribs and expelled his breath.

"Grawr." It would appear his mother wasn't dead, but she was striped and bleeding in a few places. She was also not the petite and cute quokka of his youth. She looked like she'd been dropped in a radioactive vat. Massive, hairy arms clutched him, squeezing hard enough his ribs protested. If she hugged him any tighter, she'd crush him.

He closed his eyes and thought of his bear. His big, solid panda bear.

Poof. The sudden shift broke his mother's hold, and he dropped to the floor in a tuck and roll. He popped to his feet and confronted the cutest, most enormous monster ever.

He rammed her, shoving her hard into the wall behind. Concrete cracked. They whirled, and it was his turn to be slammed against an immovable surface.

As part of the ceiling let go, tumbling down in a mess of plaster and wires, Jakob roared. "Grawr!" Which he hoped Maisy understood as "Get Peach out of here!"

He didn't have time to watch and see if they got to safety as he wrestled his mother for control. Both of them big and strong, but Jakob was holding back, even though he had a few openings to land a killing shot.

This evil villain was still his mom. Would he ever recover if he killed her?

His indecision led to him standing face to face with his mother. She flexed her claws, and he'd swear her cute furry face—the only thing still adorable and recognizable in her mutant new form—smiled.

The quokka's big, expressive eyes rounded as it exhaled a soft, "Coo?" before slumping and falling over in a furry heap.

Behind her stood his dad, a gun in one hand and an empty syringe in the other. "She really should stop hitting the 'roids."

If he could have laughed, he would have, but the moment was too grave. He and his da stared at each other. Did his dad know it was him?

As a bear, he couldn't speak, and before he could change, more Joneses filled the hall. More eyes widened. Someone said his name.

The moment he'd feared had arrived. His family now knew his secret.

It was Uncle Kary who broke the silence. "Do you know what kind of jobs and money we can make in Asia with a panda on our team?"

Nothing more was said because that was when they all heard a roared, "Miranda! Kelly! Where are you?"

The squeals of happiness could be heard by anyone, but what had everyone stunned to silence was the wail of a baby.

They ran at that point and were in time to see Chase cradling his newborn son, whom he held a loft with a grin. "He looks just like me."

Meaning the baby sported a scowl. The now bigger family huddled together, with Kelly tucked to her mom with one hand outstretched to hold the baby's hand. Miranda, still for once, beamed fondly at her mate, and Chase looked as if he'd die of happiness.

Jakob glanced to Maze on one side of him and felt the reassuring weight of a cub clinging to his back. Could they have the same thing?

When Peach hopped off to check out the baby, Jakob shifted and stupidly said to Maze, "Marry me."

16

THE DEMAND TOOK her by surprise. And she didn't answer. Couldn't. Her mouth was too dry, her heart racing like mad.

"I have to check on the baby." An excuse so she wouldn't have to answer. What would she say? Yes. But what of her fear that Jakob would leave? His uncle had made it plain that Jakob was more of an asset than ever.

Could she really be with someone who constantly went off fighting other people's wars? She'd made a vow to save lives. Unless it affected her daughter's life. She already knew she'd kill to keep her cub safe.

"Down." Peach squirmed to be let loose.

Maisy didn't want to let Peach go, but she also couldn't hold her daughter back because of fear. She set Peach on her feet. "Don't go too far."

A request that fell on deaf ears. Now that her daughter had been saved, she was more interested in the men toting guns. Peach and Kelly raced off with the Jones men, armed with enough firepower to take over a small country. She knew her kid would be safe and perhaps even of aid in reassuring the children they freed. Thirty-three of them when all was said and done, plus another dozen or so adults, nine of them former humans. Hopefully the last that would be genetically modified.

Mother Q's empire of evil was no more.

Everyone was safe once more. Jakob blushed and beamed as his family ribbed him about his panda. It pleased her to see they didn't reject him as he'd feared. On the contrary, the uncles and brothers were already talking about their future missions as they headed to the building entrance where transportation awaited them.

The Joneses headed for the helicopter with its whirring blades. Rather than watch Jakob leave with his family, Maisy, with Peach holding her hand, followed Chase, who carried Miranda, who held the baby, while Kelly sat perched on his broad shoulders.

The dust in her eyes brought tears as the chopper lifted. When the breeze died, she realized someone walked by her side. She glanced over to see Jakob.

"What are you doing?" she asked as he held open the door of the van. "Shouldn't you have gone with your family?"

"I am."

She stumbled getting into the van. He steadied her.

"I never replied to your proposal."

"Even if you never do, my place is by your side." He sat in a chair by a console and pulled her into his lap. Peach clambered over to a different chair and shared it with Kelly.

Maisy leaned her head on him. "You'll get bored pretty quick."

"You will never bore me. Marry me."

"I don't know."

It wasn't easy to say yes, even as her heart screamed at her. They returned to the Academy, and she walked around in a daze, hearing the students cheering their safe return, the school song being bellowed as they celebrated.

"Give me an F."

"F."

"U."

"U," they echoed.

"C."

"K," the group echoed with laughter.

"What does that spell?"

"Fuck."

"And what are you gonna do?"

"Fuck you!" The poem was nonsensical and ribald, also perfect for the moment, as it lightened it.

The party lasted for hours, and Maisy was still in a quandary as she tucked Peach into bed and then sat beside it.

"Say yes, Mommy."

"To what, fuzz?"

"Jakob. I want him as my daddy."

"I don't know, fuzz."

"I do." A sage gaze caught hers. "We can trust him, Mommy."

She wanted to believe. She kept hold of Peach's hand, watching as her breath evened as she fell asleep, unable to leave her side.

Which was where Jakob joined her. He said nothing, just sat at her feet and leaned on her. The chair creaked in protest.

Eventually she said, "We'd have to live somewhere with a school for Peach."

"And a soccer team. Always thought I'd make a fine coach, and she's just the right age to teach."

"I'll understand if you need the occasional break." Because it wouldn't be fair for her to ban him completely from ever doing stuff with his family.

"Nothing too dangerous or too long. If at all. After all, I've got different priorities now. I love you, Maze, and I'm just sorry it took me this long to figure out what was really important in life."

Rather than reply to his words, she let go of Peach's hand. "I need a shower." Standing, she took a few steps before stopping to look over her shoulder. "You coming?"

He did. In her mouth as she knelt before him under the hot spray then again, buried balls deep inside her. Naked bodies entwined, hearts racing together.

Bright and early the next day, Peach came bouncing in crowing, "Morning!"

She pounced them both, demanding a hug and kiss before snuggling between them.

Only when she settled did Maze tell her the news. "Jakob asked me to marry him. I hope it's okay I said yes."

Her cub let out a squeal of excitement, but when Jakob said, "Can I be your daddy?" her brave tiger roared, and her heart burst.

A panda and a kitty, finally getting their happily ever after.

EPILOGUE

THEY DIDN'T BREAK ground on the new Down Under Academy until two weeks after Mother Q was put behind bars. It would be months—more than likely up to a year—before they could move into their new home with Jakob as the professor of stealthy arts, Jax as their know-it-all when it came to cryptozoology, Uncle Kary as the dean, and his brothers and other uncles as special guests that would pop in to teach the occasional new trick. They would be hiring other people, too. Retired FUC agents who had something to teach. They might even lube an ASS or two with sweet contract deals.

Until Jakob and his family could move into their new digs, he and Maisy were working for ARSHOL, which caused his brothers no end of amusement. Yet he'd never been happier.

Maisy had lost the guarded look in her eyes when she looked at him, and her bright smiles made his day. Peach took to calling him Papa Bear, which, for some reason, made a few people choke. And when it was explained what it meant in certain circles, he blushed.

Course, he didn't mind it so much when Maisy whispered, "Ignore what they say. I think you make a fine papa bear. Now come to bed."

Heck yeah. If there was one thing this panda never said no to it was a cuddle with his kitty. They'd been through a lot and come out the other end a little bit scarred, but stronger for their experiences.

They married on campus, with Peach as their flower girl, Jakob's new half-sister as a shy bridesmaid, and his uncles wiping a few tears as they all took credit for how he turned out.

The whole FUC gang turned out, old friends and new, to celebrate a world finally free of Mastermind and copycats.

Shifters could breathe easily once more. Their secret was safe. Now they could—

"Joey escaped!"

The sudden shout saw the music halting, and people on the makeshift dance floor in the middle of the cafeteria stilled.

It took one little flower girl fist pumping and yelling, "FUCN'A to the hunt," for clothes to go flying and animals to burst into fur, feather, and even leathery skin.

But not Jakob. He turned his wife into his arms as everyone ran off to hunt down crazy wild-eyed Joey—who'd apparently not been taking his meds like a good lizard.

Jakob had no need to go chasing danger, not anymore. He had what he needed right here in his arms, which was why he kissed his new wife. Not long enough, considering it was their wedding night.

But he had more than one priority now, such as wrangling his new daughter, who went streaking past, ready to save the world.

"I'll be right back," he said with one more quick kiss.

"Papa Bear to the rescue," his wife said with a giggle.

To which he uttered a big panda, "Grawr."

THE END

For now, but there are more stories coming! Because I've always been curious, I asked some author friends if they would like to write some stories based on my FUC world. As you can imagine, some of them had some interesting tales to tell. I do hope you'll check out the new FUC Academy books and giggle as you fall in love.

LOOKING FOR THE ENTIRE F.U.C COLLECTION BY EVE LANGLAIS?